P9-CDA-738

GIVE-A-DAMN
JONES

GIVE-A-DAMN JONES

BILL PRONZINI

A Tom Doherty Associates Book

New York

GIVE-A-DAMN JONES

A Forge Book
Published by Tom Doherty Associates
175 Fifth Avenue
New York, NY 10010

www.tor-forge.com

Forge® is a registered trademark of Macmillan Publishing Group, LLC.

The Library of Congress Cataloging-in-Publication Data is available upon request.

ISBN 978-0-7653-9439-2 (hardcover)
ISBN 978-0-7653-9440-8 (ebook)

Our books may be purchased in bulk for promotional, educational, or business use. Please contact your local bookseller or the Macmillan Corporate and Premium Sales Department at 1-800-221-7945, extension 5442, or by email at MacmillanSpecialMarkets@macmillan.com.

First Edition: May 2018

Printed in the United States of America

0 9 8 7 6 5 4 3 2 1

In memory of Lawrence Davidson,
good friend and longtime Western fan

BUTTE, MONTANA

OWEN HAZARD

Well, I guess I know Give-a-Damn Jones about as well as any man ever did or could. Our paths have crossed half a dozen times over a span of years, in six different states and territories, and whenever that happens we just naturally gravitate to each other and spend a fair amount of time gambling, carousing, and swapping stories tall and true. We mostly share the same taste in food, liquor, cards, and women, and the same general notions on how type should be set and newspapers run.

Itinerant hand-peggers is what Jones and I are and have been most of our adult lives. The fiddle-footed breed known as tramp printers, though the word "tramp" translates to "shiftless" in the minds of some and we're anything but when we're at our work. Nobody ever toiled harder for wages than a type-slinger does for his. The difference between men like us and the general population is that we're not the settling-down kind. After a few days or weeks in one town, why, we get a restless urge for new places, new horizons. And once we hear the call of the open road, we're off first chance we get.

I first met Jones in Butte, Montana, in the early summer of '89. I came in by train, the way most of us traveled, riding blind baggage on the Utah and Northern Union Pacific. Didn't matter how you came to Butte, though, whether by train or stage or wagon or on horseback—you smelled it before you saw it. The air was so poisonous thick with smoke and sulphur and arsenic fumes from roasting ore pouring out of the copper mines' smelter stacks that no vegetation was left anywhere in or near the town. The pall got so heavy on windless days it blotted the sky and lamps had to be lit at midday.

The foul air, and the town's location on a steep hill-side overlooking a bare butte, were two reasons it was called the "Perch of the Devil." A third, the one that had drawn me, was that it was a wide-open boom camp, re-putedly the wildest in the west, with scores of saloons and gambling halls and houses of pleasure open twenty-four hours, same as the mines. A sin-ugly town in more ways than one, but I was only twenty-four then, just two years on the road, and hungry for as much sport as I could find.

Butte had two daily newspapers, the *Inter-Mountain* and the *Miner,* but I didn't head for either shop straight-away. First things first. I'd been told that a gent named Dublin Dan ran a saloon at Porphyry and Main that catered to the hobo trade, and that he kept a big kettle of stew boiling on a potbellied stove and permitted sleeping on the floor free of charge to any wandering roadster on his uppers. I was on mine just then, my last meal a dim memory and one thin dime left in my purse.

Give-a-Damn Jones was in Dublin Dan's when I walked in late afternoon, sitting by himself at a table reading a book. I didn't recognize him at first, didn't pay attention to him at all until after I showed my International Typesetters Union card to the barkeep and got invited to help myself to the free stew. The place was some crowded and there was room at Jones's table, so I took my bowl over there and asked could I sit with him. He looked me over, took note of my ink-stained fingers—not nearly as ink-stained as his—and said to help myself to a chair.

"How's work in town?" I asked as I parked myself.

"I've only been here a week," he said, "but *Inter-Mountain*'s hiring. Might be able to get on there if you're a good hand with a composing stick."

"Well, I'm no blacksmith," I said, "blacksmith" being what they called a typesetter who did poor work. "Never had any complaints yet."

"How many types can you pull a minute?"

"Two hundred or better."

"Without mistakes?"

"Clean as a whistle." Well, most often at that time, anyway.

"You'll do then. What's your name, sonny?"

I didn't much care for the "sonny," but then he was a good ten years older than me so I took it without comment. I told him my name and he said his was Artemas Jones.

Well, that made me sit up and take a different look at him. He was a broad-coupled, belly-lean man with long flax-colored hair, and he had the deep-set smoke-colored eyes and clean-shaven face I'd heard talked about on the road. A sort of quiet, watching and listening face. By that I mean you could tell from it, if you looked close enough, that not much passed him by that he didn't take notice of—people, places, events, all sorts of things big and little. Life in general, you might say.

"Give-a-Damn Jones," I said with a touch of awe.

A muscle fluttered under one of his eyes, almost a wince. "I've been called that. Can't say I care for it much."

"From what I hear you've earned it."

"I've known plenty of men it'd sit better on than me. And don't believe everything you hear—half of it's bound to be sheep dip."

"Too many have sung your praises for the stories not to be true, Mr. Jones."

"What stories?"

"Why, that you're always willing to help folks in need or trouble. That you can't abide injustice, can't step aside from it no matter what—"

He made a snorting sound. "Sheep dip."

"You mean you *don't* give a damn?"

"Sure I do. Any man worth his freedom ought to. But I'm no saint by a long shot, no do-gooder on the lookout like some make me out to be. I can't help it if now and then I end up in the wrong place at the wrong time."

"Or the right place at the right time."

"Point is other people's troubles keep dogging me. I don't go looking for 'em, they just come crawling my way. You understand the distinction?"

I wasn't about to argue with him. "Yes, sir. Whatever you say."

"Oh, hell. Go on, eat your stew."

He opened up his book again while I emptied my bowl. When I was done feeding I asked, "What's that you're reading, Mr. Jones?"

"Call me Artemas. Shakespeare's sonnets. You ever read Shakespeare, Owen?"

"No. Never had much time for reading."

"Man can always find time for reading if he cares to better himself. There's a wealth of things you can learn from Mr. Shakespeare. Increase your vocabulary, too."

"I know enough words now from all the type I've set."

That brought a wry chuckle. "You could live to a hundred and five with a gray beard down to your gonads and you'd still never know enough words. Or enough of anything else, either."

Good advice. But I was too young and too brash then to take it to heart.

Well, he took me under his wing and introduced me to the foreman at the *Inter-Mountain,* and not only got me hired, but given an advance on my wages—a five-dollar gold piece that bought me a comfortable room in the transients' boardinghouse where he was lodging. The

Inter-Mountain was owned by A. J. Davis, said to be the richest man in Butte, and he paid more than scale. It was the best job I'd ever had up to that point in my travels.

What made it even better was a gimmick Jones, who had a puckish sense of humor among his other virtues, and one of the home-guard printers devised. The saloon upstairs from the *Inter-Mountain* had made the mistake of running its beer pipes through a corner of the composing room, and the pair conspired and then commenced to tap and plug the pipe. Free beer on tap any time we wanted it. The proprietor of the saloon never caught on, leastways not while I was working for A. J. Davis's sheet.

I had the best sport of my life that spring, too, when we weren't working at our trade. Jones and me haunted the north side of Galena Street, the "line" in Butte—King & Lowrie's saloon and gambling palace, Pete Hanson's Clipper Shades in the heart of the red-light district, a combination dance hall, saloon, prize-fight arena, theater, and brothel called the Casino, and Molly Demurska's fancy parlor house with the prettiest girls in town. More than one morning we had the fantods from too much liquor and too little sleep, but we never missed a single minute's work in the composing room.

You couldn't ask for a better companion and mentor than Give-a-Damn Jones during the five-plus weeks we spent together in Butte. He'd been a roadster and gay cat, as we're sometimes called, for more than a dozen years and had a storehouse of stories and anecdotes that he'd regale you with when the mood struck him. He was a fount of opinions, quotations, professional gossip, place descriptions, and capsule biographies of men and women he'd known in his travels. Yet he was reticent about his family background, wouldn't say where he was born and raised or from whom he'd learned the printing trade. The only times I knew him to be rude and profane were when I attempted to draw him out. And while he shared our breed's liking for alcohol and ladies of easy virtue, he drank no more than a few beers while on the job and was unfailingly courtly to women of every stripe.

He'd traveled all over the west and back again three or four times since the age of fourteen, and worked for more than a few of the legends of newspapering: Joseph Pulitzer on the *St. Louis Post-Dispatch,* Edward Rosewater, the fighting editor of the *Omaha Bee,* and the beaver-hatted old firebrand J. West Goodwin, of the *Daily Bazoo* in Sedalia.

For a time he traveled with Hi-Ass Hull, considered the king of tramp printers for his union-organizing work, whose nickname came from a Northwest Indian word meaning "tall man." For another period he'd run with the band of roaming typographers known as the Missouri River Pirates, who frequented the towns along the Missouri River between St. Louis and Sioux City. Met Jesse James when the outlaw was living in St. Joseph under his Tom Howard alias, two days before the dirty little coward Bob Ford fired a .45 slug into Jesse's back. Others whose paths he crossed were Bat Masterson, Texas Jack

Omohundro, the poet Walt Whitman, himself a vagabond printer, and the acid-tongued writer Ambrose Bierce.

He admitted to having had no formal education, but he was a learned fellow nonetheless. By his own estimate he'd read more than two hundred books—the Bible, most of Shakespeare, and the likes of Hawthorne, Melville, and Mark Twain. He could be induced to quote passages from the Book and the Bard when in his cups, and I had no doubt they were as flawless as his typesetting. He liked music, too, just about any kind. Played a variety of tunes himself on the mouth organ, with more enthusiasm than skill.

Now it may seem that I've painted a romanticized picture of Give-a-Damn Jones. That he was too footloose, too devil-may-care to have done at least some of the good works he was credited with, and that I'm guilty of a kind of hero worship. Well, none of that is true. Within his province he was and is an honest, honorable, obliging, and downright companionable fellow.

One thing that happened during our time together in Butte proved to me that he deserved his moniker. We were on our way out of one of the gambling halls concealed behind the stores that lined China Alley when we heard a man cussing and a woman screaming in one of the side passages. By the light of a lantern over a doorway we could see a drunken miner beating on a young Chinese prostitute half his size. Jones didn't waste a second rushing to the girl's aid. He pulled the drunk off her, fetched him a poke that knocked him halfway across the alley. The miner came up on his feet with a knife in his hand, but he didn't try to use it because by then he was looking down the barrel of a revolver cocked and ready to fire. He turned tail and ran.

That was the first I knew Jones carried a pistol tucked inside one of the tall boots he wore. Most of us roadsters kept a weapon of some kind handy for self-protection, mostly barlow knives and derringers, but Jones is the only one I've ever known to pack a pistol—a Smith & Wesson Model 2 single-action, top-break, .38-caliber, five-shot revolver. He preferred it to other makes, he said, because of its size—it had a three-and-a-half-inch barrel and fit snugly into his boot—and because it was reliably accurate at close quarters. I asked him how often he'd had occasion to fire it, if he ever had, but he refused to say one way or the other.

By the end of our fifth week together I was content to stay on in Butte a while longer, but Jones was ready to move on. I could see the restless itch in him even though he didn't give voice to it. What finally sent him back on the road was a big pot he won in a draw poker game at the Clipper Shades—some forty dollars in cash and, of all things, a horse and saddle from a gent who threw in everything he owned on the strength of trip aces, only to find out Jones was holding a diamond flush.

The horse wasn't much and neither was the saddle, and I expected Give-a-Damn to sell them both for what he could get. But no. Like the rest of us type-slingers his usual mode of travel was by train, boxcar, or blind baggage, but the novelty of heading off on horseback to his next job, wherever it might be, appealed to his sense of adventure. He hadn't seen much of Montana before coming to Butte, and he figured horseback was a good way to get the lay of the Big Sky country. He told me that after the poker game, and the next morning he was gone.

It was a while before I found out where he went, for I left Butte myself not long afterward and went down to Cheyenne for a short stay and then on to points east. But stories get around quick on the road, especially when they involve a man like Give-a-Damn Jones, and it wasn't long before his name came up. And in bits and pieces, the tale of what happened to him in Box Elder, a small eastern Montana cow and farm town.

Yes, sir, that moniker of his fits right and proper. Just ask the folks in and around Box Elder . . .

BOX ELDER,
MONTANA

JADA KINCH

I didn't like Artemas Jones from the first minute I laid eyes and ears on him. For one thing, the main thing, he was riding bold as you please on posted land belonging to Colonel Elijah Greathouse. For another he was a hobo drifter—you could tell that from the weather-stained blanket coat and lye-colored pants he wore, the spavined orange dun he was riding, and the bindle sack tied behind the cantle of a broke-down Mother Hubbard saddle. And for a third he was blowing loud into a damn mouth organ. I can't abide them things. What comes out of 'em ain't music, it's squally noise like the bawling of a newborn calf.

It was late afternoon and me and Collie Burns and one of our newer hands, Al Yandle, had spent most of the day chousing strays out of brush-choked coulees along Big Creek. Better work, even so, than mending fences and checking penned cattle for disease, which was what we were mostly stuck with doing these days. I heard the noise this Jones was making before we come up out of a snaggle of chokecherry onto the main ranch road, driving a young brindle heifer that had wandered in there and trapped itself. And there he was, coming 'round a bend in the road.

Collie said, "Who the hell is that?"

"Nobody I ever saw before," Yandle said. "Can't be one of them sodbusters. None of 'em would have the gall."

"Trespassing, whoever he is," I said. I adjusted the hang of the holstered Peacemaker on my hip, laid my hand on its stag handle. "I'll find out. You boys wait here."

The trespasser pulled up and quit his caterwauling when he seen me spurring toward him. Wasn't armed as far as I could tell—no saddle gun, no sidearm. That hunk of crowbait he was forking shied some when I yanked my pony down in front of him. It was so swaybacked its belly near touched the ground. Looked as though one man pushing on its hindquarters and another on its head could fold it up in the middle like a gate hinge.

"Afternoon," he said, amiable.

"You got bad eyesight, mister?" I said. "Or can't you read plain English?"

"What do you mean?"

"What the hell you think I mean? This here's Square G land, posted land. Sign plain as day at the road fork two miles back."

"Oh. My mistake. I must've misread the sign."

"Yeah, you sure must've. What you want here?"

"I don't want anything," he said. He shifted position in the saddle, wincing the way a man does when he's not used to riding and develops butt sores. "I'm just passing through."

"Wouldn't be going to see somebody the other side of the Knob?"

"No. What's the Knob?"

I swung my arm up toward the round-topped butte that marked the north boundary of Colonel Greathouse's range. "Right up there, plain as day."

"I don't know anybody around here," he said.

"What's your name? Where you from?"

"Jones, Artemas Jones. From half a hundred places, the last one Butte."

"Don't look like a man hunting work."

He shrugged. "I am if the job's right."

"You're no cowhand, that's for sure," I said. "What kind of work you do, if any? Wood-chopping? Swamping?"

"Compositor."

"Say which?"

"Typesetter. Traveling printer." Jones flattened his hand out into a streak of sunlight to show the ink stains on his fingers.

"The hell," I said. "Never seen one of your kind on horseback before."

"I won this animal and saddle in a poker game three nights ago."

"That so? Appears to me you'd of been better off if you'd thrown in your hand."

"Well, I decided to have a look at parts of the Territory I'd never seen before, but I guess I'm not cut out for this kind of travel. Or this kind of open prairie country. Three days and nights and I've learned my lesson." He showed his teeth in a lopsided fool's grin. "I don't plan on keeping the beast for long, just until I get someplace where I can sell him. What's the nearest town on the railroad and how far?"

"Box Elder. Seven miles southeast."

"Does Box Elder have a newspaper?"

"It does, but I wouldn't think about looking for work there if I was you. Will Satterlee's the last editor you want to hire on with."

"Why is that?"

I fixed Jones with a hard eye. "He's a bullheaded troublemaker, that's why. Made an enemy of the man I ramrod for."

"How so?"

"Never mind how so. That's none of your lookout."

"He sounds like a firebrand, this editor."

"The sort that'll get himself burned if he don't back off. You don't want no part of him or his paper, not if you're smart. Just make your sale and hop the first north or south freight out of Box Elder."

"I'll keep that in mind. Mind if I ask your name?"

"Why? You'll never see me again, long as you get off Square G land and stay off."

"I like to know who's giving me advice."

"That some kind of smart-ass remark?"

"Wasn't meant to be. I'm just curious, that's all."

"Kinch. Jada Kinch."

"Well, Mr. Kinch, I apologize for the inadvertent trespass and I'll be off Square G land as quick as I can."

"See that you are. And learn how to read a signpost proper so you don't make the same mistake again."

He gave me a little salute, wheeled the crowbait around, and trotted off the way he'd come. I watched him out of sight around the bend before I rode back to where Collie and Yandle were waiting.

"Kind of a long palaver," Collie said. "Who is he, Jada?"

"Nobody," I said. "Just a half-wit tramp printer. Nobody at all."

R. W. SATTERLEE

I was in the front section of the *Banner* office, taking notes from the widow Coombs for a Saturday church social announcement, when the long-haired, rough-dressed stranger came in off the boardwalk. A blast of summer heat blew in with him, along with the loud rumble of a Murphy wagon loaded with kegs from Steinhaur's Brewery in Billings bound for the Occidental House across Central Street.

He took off his hat and stood quiet, mopping his face with a handkerchief, until my business with Mrs. Coombs was done and she walked out. She cast him a sideways glance on the way, and then sniffed as if she found him odorous and disreputable. I sure didn't. I had an idea what he was and why he was there even before he came up and gave his breed's standard opener. I was glad to see him, and Dad would be, too—if the fellow was qualified. In a small town like ours, we had a hard time getting and keeping help.

"How's work?"

"Available," I said, "if you have experience."

"More than twelve years now."

"Then you'll be welcome. The last printer we had, an oldster named Charlie Weems, left more than two months ago."

"Charlie Weems. Well, well."

"You know him?"

"Sure. Not a tooth left in his head, but he still chews tobacco and can ring a spittoon at twenty yards. Only one eye, claims to have lost the other in an explosion of a Queen Anne musket. Drinks forty-rod whiskey, can recite the names and addresses of most houses of ill repute he's ever visited, talks a blue streak while he sets type, and boasts that since he turned seventy he hasn't spent more than a week at any job in any town."

"He set type pretty fast for a man his age."

"Fastest ever when he was young, to hear him tell it. How many pages in your sheet?"

"Four. Only two now and then, when there isn't enough news and advertisements to fill. We go to press early Thursday morning and circulate that afternoon. And we're behind schedule for this week."

"Standard union wages?"

"Sure. Twenty-five cents a thousand ems."

His gray eyes took my measure. "I'd say you're too young to be the owner of a territorial newspaper. No offense."

"None taken. I just passed my seventeenth birthday. My father, Will Satterlee, is the owner."

"I believe I've heard the name. And you'd be Will junior?"

"No. Robert William Satterlee. But everyone calls me R.W."

"You'll go places, then," he said. "Men who use their initials often do."

I asked for his name.

"Jones. Artemas Jones."

"Give-a-Damn Jones?"

"So I've been called. How do you know the moniker? Charlie Weems?"

"Yes, sir. He mentioned you a couple of times. But he didn't say how you came by it."

"Nor will I." Short and a touch sharp, as if he were embarrassed by the explanation. "I prefer to be called Artemas. Your father on the premises?"

"Over to the marshal's office, hunting news about Jim Tarbeaux. He should be back before long."

"Who would Jim Tarbeaux be?"

Maybe I shouldn't have answered as readily as I did, but Charlie Weems had spoken highly of Give-a-Damn Jones and there was something about him that made him easy to talk to. Besides, it was all right there in the back issues of the *Banner*.

"Man just released from Deer Lodge," I said. "He used to live here in the basin and some folks don't like the idea of him coming back."

"Hard case?"

"Not five years ago, when he was convicted of grand theft. Just pretty wild. But he could be now, I guess. They say prison hardens a man."

"I've known one it did and two it didn't. Mind telling me something else, R.W.?"

"If I can."

"I took a wrong turn on my way here and ended up on Square G land. A fellow named Kinch advised me not to stop in Box Elder and ask for work. He said your father had made an enemy of the Square G's owner."

"Colonel Elijah Greathouse," I said. "A very important man in the basin, or used to be."

"Used to be?"

"Before he lost most of his cattle the bad winter before last, along with just about every other rancher hereabouts— what folks call the 'Great Die-Up' or the 'Big Die.' The Square G is still the largest, and he's still head of the Cattlemen's Association, but he's not as powerful as he once was. He can't rebuild his herd because prices are low and he can't get a loan, and he hates the German and Scandinavian farmers from Wisconsin and Minnesota who are taking over what used to be open grazing land."

"Trouble between him and the farmers?"

"Yes." I probably should have let it go at that, but Dad says I have a tendency to run off at the mouth, and besides, if Give-a-Damn Jones was going to work for us, he needed to know how things stood. So I went on, "The farmers aren't squatters, the land was deeded to them free and clear, but the Colonel hates them just the same. He thinks they have been butchering cows of his that wandered through fence breaks onto their tracts, or that the nesters broke the fences themselves and have been rustling the steers. But he can't prove it. There have been a few night raids on the settlers' tracts recently—masked riders tearing down their fences, shooting a few animals and a flock of chickens. My father believes the Colonel is responsible."

"And has written editorials accusing him of it."

"Yes. Others critical of the Colonel, too."

I didn't add that the editorials had been increasingly fiery, denouncing Colonel Greathouse as a hidebound despot who refused to accept the fact that Montana was changing, becoming more populated, more settled, and that the glory days of cattle ranching had ended with the devastating winter of '86–'87. I agreed. So did a lot of other folks in Box Elder, and more importantly, so did the Territorial Legislature in Helena. Word was that we would be ratified as the forty-first state in the Union next year.

I also didn't say anything about how concerned I was about the escalating conflict between Dad and Colonel Greathouse. Will Satterlee is a fine man, a good father, but he has an iron will and his convictions are unshakable when he believes he is in the right. If he kept goading the Colonel the way he had been, I was afraid their feud would erupt into violence. It could happen, especially now that Jim Tarbeaux was out of prison and likely to return to Box Elder. Dad was convinced that Tarbeaux had been railroaded, and the Colonel's harsh disapproval of Tarbeaux's former relationship with his daughter, Mary Beth, made the hostility even more volatile.

"Well," I said, "now that you know how things stand, Mr. Jones—"

"Artemas."

"—do you still want to work for us? We could sure use help getting out this week's issue. And with all the job printing we've got piled up."

"You'll have it, if your father approves my hiring. And maybe for a while after that."

"Oh, he'll approve. Surely he will."

"Well, then. Suppose you show me around your shop while we wait for him."

He came through the gate at the end of the counter, and I led him into the rear section of the shop and stood by while he eyed our cranky old hand press, soapstone table, forms, type frames and cases, stacks of newsprint, and inking material.

"Albion," he said, nodding at the skeleton shape of the press. "Harks back to Horace Greeley's day at the *New York Tribune*."

"Dad wants to replace it with a newer Washington press, but we can't afford it right now."

Artemas examined the Albion and allowed as how it appeared to be in reasonably good shape. Then he opened upper- and lower-case type drawers and nodded approvingly at the selection of Revier, nonpareil, and agate.

Another approving nod followed his study of the previous week's issue from a leftover bundle.

"This is tolerable good for a jim-crow sheet," he said.

"What's a jim-crow sheet?"

He grinned. "Small-town newspaper. Your father's been in the game a while, I take it."

"Eight years in Box Elder. Before that four years in Laramie, and before that stints in Sacramento and Marysville, where I was born."

"I like working for an editor who knows his business. And who isn't afraid to stand up for what he believes in." Artemas paused and added with a little quirk of his mouth, "Even when I've been advised against it."

SETH JENNISON

I like Will Satterlee, I admire his moxie, and more often than not I agree with his point of view, but sometimes he gives me a sharp pain in my hindquarters. Today was one of those times.

He'd come in to ask if I'd heard anything more about Jim Tarbeaux coming home to Box Elder—I hadn't, not a word since Tarbeaux's release from Deer Lodge four days ago—and then he started in on his favorite topic, the sins of Colonel Elijah Greathouse. He'd worked himself up into a tirade, stomping around my office like a fighting cock on the strut. Fighting cock was a good description of him—bantam-sized, head bobbing, beak of a nose thrust out, jowls a-quiver, tufts of feathery gray hair poking out every which way.

I tried to calm him down, reminding him of his high blood pressure, but he wouldn't calm. "Greathouse is a pox on this community," he kept saying, "and you know it as well as I do. He's had his own way too long. Deviling those immigrant farmers, doing everything in his power to drive them off land that legally belongs to them and keep others from settling, and he'll devil Jim Tarbeaux, too."

"Likely Tarbeaux won't stay long when he comes back," I said. "Just long enough to sell his ranch."

"He may decide to stay on at Keystone instead of selling it."

"Uh-huh. Eight months now since his pa died, and what few cattle George had left sold at auction and the money gone to pay taxes. Take money to fix it up, get it working again. He wouldn't dare use what's left of that fifty-four hundred dollars he stole."

"Don't start in on that again, Seth. That money has been long spent, and not a dime of it by him."

"Have it your way. If he does put the ranch up for sale, he won't get much the way things are now. Might not get anything at all." A fat blowfly buzzed my ear, and I took a swipe at it and missed. Blasted flies. Worst summer for flies and mosquitoes since the blistering hot one of '86.

"There is another reason he might stay," Will said. "Mary Beth Greathouse."

"Her still being unspoken for don't mean she's been waiting five years for Tarbeaux."

"Yes it does. Why else would she keep resisting the attentions of every eligible male within fifty miles? And I happen to know she wrote him letters the entire time he was in prison."

"She did? How'd she'd manage that, the way the Colonel feels about Tarbeaux?"

"A resourceful woman can always find a way."

"Uh-huh. How'd you find out about those letters?"

"I have my sources. Reliable sources."

"Uh-huh. And you figure her and Tarbeaux will take up again."

"I do. Assuming he still cares for her as much as she does for him, and I have no reason to believe otherwise."

"The Colonel won't stand for it."

"That's what worries me. That profane, half-senile old buzzard did all he could to break up their romance before the robbery. Now he's doubly convinced Tarbeaux isn't good enough for his daughter. It would never even occur to him that the man was wrongly convicted."

"Will," I said, "you're the only one still believes Tarbeaux didn't steal that money in spite of all the evidence stacked against him."

"Hang the evidence. Built on foolish behavior and a string of lies. And I am not the only one who believes in his innocence. Mary Beth surely does."

"Maybe so, but the Colonel—"

"Hang the Colonel, too. You know as well as I do that he's liable to do something drastic—frame Tarbeaux for another crime or burn him out if he stays at Keystone. And if he and Mary Beth should run off together, I wouldn't put it past him to have Tarbeaux shot."

"Oh, now, he wouldn't go that far. Man's ruthless, I grant you, but he'd never sink to murder."

"Don't be too sure of that."

"Now, Will—"

"He didn't dirty his own hands during the war and he has never dirtied them here that can be proven, but he's quite capable of stooping to any sort of crime to further his own interests, murder included. And that ramrod of his, Kinch, would carry it out."

"Pshaw. Kinch may be hard-nosed, but he's no gun-slick."

"Would you stake your life on that, Seth? I wouldn't stake mine."

Much as I hated to admit it, Will had a point. About the Colonel, if not necessarily about Jada Kinch. Great-house was a hard man with a fierce temper and questionable scruples, no getting around that. Hardly liked or much respected in Box Elder, but he still had power and political clout and most folks were chary if not down-right afraid of him. I wasn't, even though he could lose me my job as town marshal if I stepped half as hard on his toes as Will Satterlee had been doing. But that didn't mean I could buck him without cause.

He'd been a brevet colonel with C Company of the Tenth Kansas Volunteers during the War Between the States, and boastful of his war record and military record—but Will had done some investigating, found out Greathouse was disliked as a bully by the soldiers under his command, and wrote one of his editorials revealing same. The two of 'em hadn't cared for each other before that, though civil enough when they met, but that editorial started their feud and subsequent ones just as fiery escalated it.

I'd tried to talk sense to Will, convince him to tone down his near-libelous attacks. So had Mayor Blevins and some of the other city fathers, even a few of the smaller cattlemen in the basin who didn't care for nesters any more than Greathouse did. But Will wouldn't listen, wouldn't step down off his soapbox. Who'd speak for the down-trodden if he didn't, he said. Well, he had a point there, too, but still . . .

I said, "What would you have me do? Tell Jim Tarbeaux he's not welcome in Box Elder and he better leave Mary Beth alone, sell out, and drift? That's what the Colonel wants. Rufus Cable, too. He's scared to death of Tarbeaux. And got a right to be, after the beating Tarbeaux gave him at the hotel and the threat he made after the trial."

"Cable is a weak-minded, deceitful fool. And a thief. I still maintain his testimony was false."

"Well, even if you're right, he believes Tarbeaux intends to do him grievous harm. But Tarbeaux's paid his debt and I got no authority to keep him from coming back here if he's a mind to, no matter his reasons or what he did and said in anger five years ago. I told Rufus that. Yes, and I told the Colonel the same. As long as Tarbeaux don't break the law again, he can go where he likes and do what he pleases in Box Elder."

"Did you warn Greathouse to leave him alone?"

"I got no authority to issue warnings outside the town limits, you know that—the Square G's county jurisdiction. He'd throw me off his property if I tried and have every right to do it."

"So you intend to do nothing at all. Just let him make trouble for Tarbeaux the way he has for Hugo Rheinmiller and the other nesters?"

My dander was up now, too. I hauled out of my desk chair and went over and looked down on Mr. Satterlee. I stand six one in my socks and the top of his rooster-feathered head come to just about my jawline. "Dammit, man, my hands are tied. Not by Colonel Greathouse, by the law. The law! Unless somebody commits a provable crime in Box Elder, there's not a blessed thing I can do except keep the peace the best way I know how."

"Greathouse is the force behind those night raids—"

"*Provable,* I said. If I had proof he's responsible, I'd notify the county sheriff quick as you can spit. But I don't and neither do you or anybody else. All you're doing with those fire-and-brimstone editorials of yours is making a bad situation worse. Stirring the pot until it's liable to boil over and scald somebody. You, probably."

"I'm not afraid of Elijah Greathouse," Will said. "He wouldn't dare harm me."

There wasn't any use in my jawing with him any more. The man was so blasted stubborn Jesus Christ himself couldn't talk sense to him. I shut my mouth and kept it shut.

But like always, he had to have the last word. "My business is to inform the people of the truth," he said in that righteous way of his, "and I intend to go on doing so. The truth shall set ye free."

And with that, he went stomping out and slammed the door behind him so hard it rattled in the frame.

HUGO RHEINMILLER

I come into town to fetch and pay for the plowshare Elrod Patch makes to replace the broken one on my plow. My youngest boy Berne comes with me and waits in the wagon while I go into the blacksmith shop.

This man Patch I would rather not have business with. He does not like men who farm the land because we are poor. Most of his trade is shoeing horses and making branding irons for the cattlemen, who are not poor or not as poor as we. He is unfriendly, a ruffian, and mean to animals. Once, I have heard, he crushed the skull of a horse with a sledgehammer when it kicked him while he was shoeing it. But he is the best blacksmith in Box Elder, and for a job such as forging a new plowshare that will not break as easily as the old one, I make the decision I must go to him.

He is at one of his forges when I walk in. A bull of a man, this Patch, his weight is as much fat as muscle. Arms thick as saplings, a tangle of brown hair, a thick mustache like a slice of sagebrush. His cowhide apron is black with soot. The shop is hot, smoky, and smells of scorched hoof and burned leather. The forges and anvils, they show how much use they have had, and the half-tubs of water used for cooling hot metal are charred around the edges. Rows of horseshoes hang from nails on the walls and the cross-beam, brands from the irons he has made are burned into the wallboards. He is proud of his workplace, I will say that in his favor.

He lifts a glowing iron shoe, a mule shoe, from the forge, lowers it into a water tub with a pair of tongs. The hiss it makes is like that of a nest of snakes. Only then does he look at me through the steam, in the way he always does—*mit Verachtung,* what Berne, who has better English than I do, translates as "disdain." Patch's thick lips bend at one corner as he says, "Come for your plowshare, Rhein-miller?"

"Yah. Yes. It is ready?"

"Over there next to that pile of old shoes."

I go over to look. The edge is honed very sharp. He has done a good job and I tell him so. Then I take the coins from the pocket of my overalls, one five-dollar gold piece and three one-dollar pieces. He puts down the tongs, wipes his hands on his apron, takes the coins from my hand.

"Where's the rest?" he says.

"The rest? There is eight dollars, as agreed."

"You got a bad memory, Rheinmiller. The price we agreed on is twelve dollars."

"Twelve! No, no, it was eight—"

"You get that figure in writing?"

"In writing? No, you told me eight, I take you at your word—"

"And my word was twelve. You want that shiny new plowshare, pony up another four bucks."

Anger turns my face hot. "I do not have four more dollars. I have only what I have just given you, eight dollars."

"Then go back to your soddy and get the rest."

"No. You are trying to cheat me by raising the price!"

"Bullshit." He rears up like the animal he is, steps toward me. "I ain't gonna stand for a Heinie dirt farmer calling me a cheat and a liar. Get the hell out of my shop or I'll throw you out."

"I will go to the marshal, tell him about this . . . this outrage."

"Go ahead, see where it gets you. Here, here's your money," and he throws the coins into the straw at my feet.

I stare down at them, my hands shaking. But what can I do except pick them up? Eight dollars is not a small sum to me, to my family. Patch watches me, laughs when I must take the five-dollar coin from a clump of manure. But there are only three coins, not four. I make sure before I face him again.

"You kept one dollar, Mr. Patch."

"That's right, I did. You come back with eleven more, you get the plowshare and our business is finished. You don't, this here dollar is for my time and trouble."

"You cannot do that, it is against the law!"

"Not when it's part of our agreement, it ain't. My word against yours, Rheinmiller."

It will do no good to argue, to call him the thief he is. I put a tight rein on my temper, return the seven dollars to my pocket, then turn from him and walk away slow with my back straight and my head high.

Behind me he says, "I don't see you again pretty soon, I got the right to sell that fine new plowshare to somebody else. Remember that."

Berne has stepped down from the wagon seat. When he sees my hands are empty and how angry I am, he knows something is wrong. And he is even more angry when I tell him what Patch has done. He wants to go into the blacksmith shop and confront the man, but I will not let him. He is only twenty, big for his age, but he is no match for a *verdammt* bull.

We drive to Marshal Jennison's office and I report to him. He has sympathy but he tells Berne and me there is nothing he can do. "Patch has pulled that kind of trick before," he says, "raising his price at the last minute when he's made something he knows he can unload to somebody else. But he's right that without a written agreement, it's your word against his, Mr. Rheinmiller."

"We can't afford to pay another four dollars right now," Berne says, "so what are we supposed to do about a new plowshare? Our old one's broken, worthless."

"About the only thing is to ask Frank Austin to make

you one. He's not half the blacksmith Patch is, but he'll bargain and he won't try to cheat you."

"An inferior plowshare and another week's work gone while we wait. It's not fair, it's not right!"

"No, it isn't."

"Somebody ought to do something about him. Fix him good."

"Might be somebody will someday. Just don't let it be you."

Berne and I go to see the other blacksmith, Frank Austin. The price we settle on for a new plowshare is seven dollars. I should have gone to him in the first place. Even if his work is not so good as Patch's, I will not be cheated or shamed by him. The throwing of my five-dollar piece into the manure, and Patch's laughter, is a *Beleidigung* I will not soon forget.

WILL SATTERLEE

As a rule I am barely tolerant of itinerant typographers. The few who have stopped in Box Elder during my time here were by and large the dregs of the breed—a scruffy, unreliable, and occasionally surly lot who vanished as suddenly as they appeared, on occasion in the midst of a job. Still, they are a necessary cog in the business of publishing a small-town newspaper, for typesetting is a dirty, time-consuming task. I have done a great deal of it over the years, and R.W. is old enough now to assist in lifting and positioning the heavy, sloping frames and pulling and setting type in the forms, but neither of us is very adept at it. The business of writing copy, page layout, and presswork is difficult enough without adding another chore.

But I must say this fellow Artemas Jones appeared to be a cut or two above the average tramp printer. Unlike any other, he had rather surprisingly arrived in town on horseback instead of by rail. He was reasonably polite, intelligent, sober, and judging by the questions he asked, interested in more than just his work, wages, and creature comforts. My only objection to him was his mildly profane nickname, but since he preferred to be addressed only by his given name, it was not an issue.

R.W. had taken to him immediately. The only other compositor I had hired whose company he enjoyed was the toothless old man Charlie Weems, and Weems had a foul mouth and a coterie of salacious stories not fit for the ears of a boy not yet seventeen at that time. Of course R.W. is at an impressionable age and thus inclined to the influence of men who have led adventurous lives, though for the most part his head sits squarely on his young shoulders. He inherited my inquisitiveness and sense of fair play—and fortunately for him, his mother's stature. Mae, God rest her soul, stood three inches taller than I and was fifteen well-placed pounds heavier; R.W. is already five inches taller and outweighs me by thirty pounds, not an ounce of it fat. A son to make a man proud . . . most of the time.

Another thing I liked about Jones was his account of the encounter with Jada Kinch. He had told R.W. about it, and in turn R.W. told me. The boy had also informed Jones of the bones of contention between Colonel Greathouse and me, and Greathouse and the settlers—matters that should not have been discussed with a stranger not yet hired. I would remonstrate with R.W. about it later. That tendency to speak out of turn to strangers is a weakness I am determined to see him outgrow.

"And you say Kinch warned you to not seek work here at the *Banner*?" I asked Jones.

"Not exactly a warning. He called it advice."

"Which you ignored. Why?"

Jones shrugged. "I don't much care to be told where I can work and for whom."

"Don't the tensions in Box Elder bother you?"

"I've been places where they ran a lot higher and hotter."

"And left in a hurry when they threatened to explode?"

"Not necessarily. I've never yet left an editor high and dry."

"How long would you be willing to remain in my employ?"

He lifted his shoulders again. "I'll be honest with you, Mr. Satterlee. Until the itch to move on strikes me. Likely not more than a couple of weeks, but not less than a full week, either. You have my word on that."

The look on my face must have told him what I thought of the word of a tramp printer, for he added, "You can withhold my wages until the end of this week to make sure I keep it. I have my poker winnings to tide me over."

This sold me completely on the man's mettle, but it being my custom to test a compositor's skill before officially hiring him, I had him set a news story I had written for the next issue, which concerned the Volunteer Fire Brigade's need for a new pump engine. Jones stood at the case frames and pulled oily ten-point type and quadrats off the case with a rattling click, justified each line the instant his brass composing stick was full, and placed it in the galley—all with unerring accuracy and at a speed that impressed me almost as much as it did R.W. When he finished, he blocked the story into a proof form and rolled out a galley for my inspection. There was not a single error or widow line.

It was mid-afternoon by then, but Jones agreed to work until five o'clock. He had eaten before coming to the *Banner* office, he said; he asked only the location of the town hostler and where he might seek lodging. R.W. directed him to Benson's Livery and to Ma Stinson's Traveler's Rest, a combination hotel and boardinghouse near the Great Northern depot that catered to railroad men, drummers, and transients. Then, with the boy's aid, he began preparing and setting the other ready copy and advertisements for Thursday's issue.

While they were at their tasks, I sat at my desk to write a new editorial. Taking care not to cross the line into libel, I skewered Colonel Elijah Greathouse even more eloquently and profoundly than ever before. I made mention again of his dubious war record, relating it to his high-handed tactics where the immigrant farmers were concerned. I called for all honest, law-abiding ranchers to oust Greathouse as president of the Cattlemen's Association before he did irreparable damage to the peace and prosperity of Box Elder.

Perhaps I went a bit too far this time, but I felt entirely justified. The man had become a destructive force in the basin, and the sooner the citizens realized it and ceased tolerating his divisive behavior, the more sane and secure our future would be.

RUFUS CABLE

I sat with my back to the wall, waiting.

Shadows shrouded the big room, thinned by early daylight filtering in through the plate-glass front window. Beyond the window I could see Main Street, mostly empty at this hour, the usual churn of dust that aggravated my lung disease and set me to coughing when I was outside. It was going to be another hot day. A thin, dry breeze rattled the chain-hung sign on the outer wall: **RUFUS CABLE, SADDLE MAKER**.

Familiar shapes surrounded me in the gloom. Workbenches littered with scraps of leather, mallets, cutters, stamping tools. A few saddles, finished and unfinished—not half as many as there had once been. Wall racks hung with bridles and hackamores, saddlebags and other accessories. Once the tools and accomplishments of my trade had given me pleasure, comfort, satisfaction. Not any longer, not since the doctor in Billings had given me the bad news. Even the good odors of new leather and beeswax and harness oil had soured in my nostrils.

It was stuffy in the shop, but I hadn't opened a window

when I came in at dawn after another sleepless night. No matter how warm it was now, how hot it would get later, I felt cold. Gut cold, the kind that had nothing to do with my illness and that no amount of heat can relieve. Yet my hands, twisted together in my lap, were sweating.

I glanced at the shotgun leaning against the wall alongside the stool. A seed-company calendar was tacked above it, next to the storeroom door, not that I needed a calendar to tell me what day this was. The date or the day of the week didn't matter—it was the fifth day since Jim Tarbeaux's release from Deer Lodge. Four long days of waiting and the fifth just starting. Would this be the one when Tarbeaux came back to Box Elder? He should have been here by now. Taking his time, savoring the moment when he would carry out his vow to end my life? Thinking to make me sweat even more?

My gaze lingered on the shotgun a few seconds longer. It had been my father's, an old double-barreled Remington that I'd brought from home when I learned of Tarbeaux's release. When he came, it would be through the front door, not the back door. Killing on the sneak wasn't his way. No, he'd want to do it face-to-face, looking me straight in the eyes.

I scrubbed my damp palms on my Levi's, then slid my turnip watch from my vest pocket, flipped the dust cover, held the dial up close to my eyes. Just eight o'clock. If I could work, it would make the time go by more quickly. The past four days I'd forced myself to cut and lay out the patterns for the saddle I was making for Paul Miller, who owned the Diamond M. The skirts, jockeys, swells, and the rest were all rigged out, ready to be assembled. I should have cased the leather yesterday, then started covering the gullet and cantle today. But I hadn't, and I wasn't sure, sitting here now, with what might be another long day stretching out ahead, that I could force myself to do any work at all. Even if I could, the saddle wouldn't come out right. My hands were too unsteady today for leather craft.

Somebody knocked loud on the door.

I jerked upright so quick I almost upset the stool, made a fumbling grab for the shotgun. The latch rattled and the door opened. I saw him through a thin haze of sweat when he came in, the Remington's twin barrels wobbling in my hands.

He wasn't Tarbeaux.

A man in a blanket coat I had never seen before, long light-colored hair curling out from under a leather cap, a beat-up Mother Hubbard saddle slung over one shoulder. He stiffened at sight of the shotgun, lifted his free hand palm forward and said, "Whoa!" I let out a ragged breath, slanted the shotgun toward the floor, then took a step backward and sagged onto the stool.

"I hope you don't greet all your customers this way, Mr. Cable."

"I'm not open for business yet." It came out as weak and shaky as my hands and knees felt.

"The owner of Benson's Livery said you open at eight."

"Not today. Who are you, mister?"

"My name's Jones. New printer at the *Banner,* on my way to work."

"What do you want?"

"I just sold my horse to Mr. Benson, but he wouldn't buy this saddle. He said you might."

"No. I've got no use for an old kak like that."

"I'll take five dollars for it. Must be worth that."

"Not to me. No."

"Four dollars?"

"I don't want it at any price."

"Know anybody who might?"

"No. Go away, leave me be."

"You feeling all right? You look a little pale—"

I had the shotgun angled across my lap and I pulled it around so the barrels were aimed his way again. "Hard of hearing? I said leave me be!"

He went, not hurrying as some might, with a glance over his shoulder that I couldn't read. He shut the door quiet behind him.

I leaned the Remington against the wall again. My face and hands felt as though I had ducked them in a pail of water. It was two or three minutes before my heart quit racing and I could breathe without tightness in my chest. Then I got up and went to do what I should have done in the first place—lock the door. I didn't want anybody other than Tarbeaux coming in the way the stranger had, not today. I thought I was ready to face Tarbeaux, but now I knew I wasn't. Let him knock if he came, when he came. Better that way because I'd have time to steady myself first.

How much longer? Christ, how much longer?

I kept on sitting with my back to the wall, waiting.

JIM TARBEAUX

The coach on the rattling, bucking four-car Great Northern spur-line train was stifling hot, none of the windows open more than a couple of inches because of the danger of flying cinders. I shifted position to ease the stiffness in my back, then leaned up to lift the window shade. The rolling prairie was familiar and I could see a portion of the river shining in the distance. Getting close. Wouldn't be long now.

Jim Tarbeaux's homecoming, I thought with some of the old bitterness. I should have let the town council know when I'd be arriving. Maybe they'd have had a brass band on hand to greet me.

The seat springs creaked as a heavy weight settled down beside me. The fat man who'd been pestering other passengers through most of the trip said through a fat smile, "Box Elder in eight minutes, by my watch."

I ignored him.

Undaunted, he said, "Bagby's my name and whiskey's my game. Fred T. Bagby, traveling representative for the Jesse Moore–Hunt Company of San Francisco. AA brand rye and bourbon whiskey and imported Scotch and Canadian whiskey my specialties. Old Crow and Thistle Dew are both excellent, but my personal favorite is O.K. Cutter. The finest rye in the nation, bar none. You've sampled it, I'm sure."

"No."

"Well, you're in for a treat when you do. Yes, sir, a real treat. Wyoming and Montana, that's my territory. I come to Box Elder once a year and always a pleasure to return. Fine little town."

I didn't say anything.

"Getting off there yourself, are you? Or traveling on to another of the river towns?"

"Getting off."

"Live there? Or stopping on business?"

"Both."

"Mind if I ask what business you're in, sir?"

"Breaking rocks the past five years," I said.

"Eh?"

"I'm an ex-convict, five days out of Deer Lodge Prison."

The fat man jerked a sideways look at me. Either what he saw in my face or what I'd said slid him off the seat, sent him away to sit with one of the upright citizens in the coach.

We were coming into the outskirts of Box Elder now. The town had grown some since I'd been away, more than I'd expected. The railroad was responsible—it had only just expanded into this part of the Territory when I was sent up, and the spur line was in the process of construction. Until '83, stagecoaches, freight wagons, and shallow-draft steamboats had been the main methods of transportation to and from Box Elder and the other small towns along the upper Missouri, Yellowstone, and Powder Rivers. There were more farms in the area, too, now, Mary Beth had written in one of her letters—parcels deeded off to homesteaders along the river and feeder creeks where once there had been nothing but rolling rangeland. Everything changes, sooner or later. Land, towns, men. Some men more than others.

I lifted my grip from the floor between my feet onto my lap, rested my hands on it as the train chuffed through switches and finally ground to a halt at the depot. I waited for the other passengers to leave before I followed, a wave of noonday heat slapping at me as I stepped off. Cattle pens stretched out on the north side of the tracks now. On the near side, the extension of town known as Shantyville seemed to have about the same number of saloons, lodging houses, and shacks. I thought ruefully of the nights I'd spent in the Ace High and the Free and Easy. That last night in particular, one I would never forget because it had been the beginning of the end of my freedom.

Mary Beth had written me that Tom Kendall died in his sleep in '85, and that Bob Kendall had lost the K-Bar after the terrible winter of '86–'87 and moved south to Laramie. I'd been sorry to hear of both. I held no hard feelings toward the Kendalls. They were no different from the rest

of the people in and around Box Elder, believing Rufus
Cable's lies and that there'd been larceny as well as kid-
wildness in me. You couldn't blame them for feeling
betrayed. Only one man was to blame and that was Cable.

The main street, Central, a continuation of the wagon
road from the northwest, slanted southeast to the river.
Nine blocks long, it ended at the bridge that'd been built
when the steamers stopped running, the wagon road picking up again on the far side. On this side, Valley Road split
off Central just before the bridge, followed the river out of
town through settled farmland, then angled across the
prairie toward the Knob; in the opposite direction a track
hooked off and dead-ended in a wide, willow-lined flat
where Fourth of July celebrations used to be held and
probably still were.

I could have avoided the business district, taken side
streets to where I needed to go, but that was the coward's
way. Walk tall and straight down Central as if I still belonged here. And maybe I did at that, no matter how much
grief it was likely to cause me if I stayed for long. Just so
none of that grief fell on Mary Beth.

I set off with my grip. The big, old box elder that had
given the town its name still sat inside its rusty metal fence
in the middle of Central, the street forking into loops
around its broad base. Some of the false-front buildings
were familiar, too: the newspaper and land offices, Occidental House saloon and gambling hall, Cattlemen's Bank,
Prairie Mercantile, Box Elder Hotel, Flowers Feed and

Grain. Over on the south side were the homes of the wealthier townspeople and the tall spire of the community church I'd seldom attended jutting into the sun-bleached sky. Many other buildings were unfamiliar. It gave me an odd, uncomfortable feeling to know this town where I was born and yet not know it—to be home and yet to understand that it could never be the same home I'd known as a boy and young man. The smart thing for me to do was to sell Pa's land, move far away—bury the past so I'd have a shot at a decent future. But not until I'd confronted Rufus Cable.

There wasn't much activity in the sweltering midday heat. Most of the few people I passed on the boardwalk, on a handful of wagons churning up powdery dust along the street, paid no attention to me. One of the loungers in the shade on the hotel veranda followed me with his eyes as I passed, but I didn't look the same as I had before Deer Lodge—leaner, no mustache, my hair a lighter brown and cut short—and he couldn't place me any more than I could place him. Another man, a ranch-hand loading sacks of flour into a linchpin wagon in front of the mercantile, gave me a long look that might have had recognition in it, but he didn't make the mistake of trying to speak to me.

My first stop was the jailhouse, on Lincoln a block off Central—still the only stone building in Box Elder, so far as I could tell. Seth Jennison was still town marshal; his name was on the door. He was at his desk inside, one foot propped up on it, fanning himself with a piece of cardboard in one hand and swatting flies with the other. The office looked just as it had the last time I'd been here—same roll-top desk, same potbellied stove, same gun rack on the wall next to the door that led into the cell block. Jennison hadn't changed much, either, except to grow a mite crag-gier and balder. He looked mild, almost indolent, but I knew from experience that when push came to shove, he was whang-leather tough.

"I just came in on the train," I said. "I thought you'd want to know."

He nodded, his expression neutral as he studied me. "Figured you'd be back. Short visit or fixing to stay?"

"I don't know yet. Haven't made up my mind."

"Your privilege, either way. Just so long as you keep your nose clean while you're here."

"As clean as folks will allow. I'm not looking for trouble."

"'Specially not with Rufus Cable."

"Don't worry, Marshal. What I said to him in court after my trial was just angry backlash."

"He thinks you meant it as a violent threat."

"I didn't."

"I sure hope not. Never did appreciate having to stir my stumps when it's this blessed hot."

I left him to his fanning and swatting and continued downstreet through the shimmers of heat. When I reached Territory Street, I looked north and picked out a chain-hung shingle just off Central that read **RUFUS CABLE,**

Saddle Maker. Mary Beth had written me that he'd bought the saddle shop, a business he'd always wanted for himself—no doubt paying for it with part of the fifty-four hundred dollars before squandering the rest. Waited until after his ma died, then claimed it was money she'd saved and he'd saved that paid for it. From where I stood I could see a Closed sign in one corner of the plate-glass front window. I would not have gone to see him even if the door had been standing wide open, not today, not yet. Patience was one of the things those years in the pen had taught me.

Benson's Livery hadn't changed any—same name, same location near the northeast wagon road, same massive hip-roofed barn set back behind a broad compound strewn with old harness and wagon rigs. Same owner and hostler, too, mossy-headed old Sam Benson. He took one look at me when he came out of the barn and said, "Well, Jim Tarbeaux. I heard you was out and might be comin' back."

"Bother you that I did?"

"Why should it? You paid your debt."

"You were on the jury, Sam."

"Sure I was," he said. "And I voted you guilty along with the rest based on the evidence. But that don't mean I was happy about it. Something I can do for you?"

"Rent me a horse and saddle."

"For how long?"

"Long enough to look over Keystone, decide what I want to do about it."

"You ain't thinking of staying on permanent?"

"Why not? I could just dig up the stolen money from where I hid it and use it to fix the place up, couldn't I?"

He just looked at me, his jaws working on a cud of blackstrap.

I said, "Does it matter to you if I stay?"

"To others, maybe, not to me." He spat onto the dusty, hoof-beaten ground. "Fifty cents a day, if you got no preference. Seventy-five cents if you pick one of the better horses. I'll settle for, oh, two dollars in advance."

"No preference. You make the choice."

The horse Benson and his helper, a copper-skinned half-breed called Robbie, picked out of the corral and saddled was a blue-tick roan that had seen better days but seemed sturdy enough. I paid Benson the two dollars, which left me with slightly more than fifty from the prison-earned pittance I'd been handed along with a cheap sack suit when I was released. I would need plenty more than that whether I stayed to make a pass at resurrecting Keystone or moved on, and where would I get it with my record? Not from Mary Beth, even if she had money of her own to offer. Somebody might give me a temporary job in town or on one of the other small ranches, but if so it would be grunt work and wouldn't pay much.

No sense in worrying over it now. Time enough for that later, too.

I rode across the bridge, passed the schoolhouse backed by a motte of cottonwoods, and on across the prairie toward the half-dozen small ranches, Keystone among them, at the upper end of the basin. The tawny blanket of summer-cured buffalo grass and clumps of sage were sparser than I remembered, and there were nowhere near as many cattle grazing as there had been in the spring of '84.

The brutal string of blizzards a year and a half ago—the worst winter the west had ever seen after a series of hot, dry summers—had devastated the heavily overstocked ranges in eastern Montana and parts of Wyoming and the Dakotas. Word was that the weeks of bitter cold and the lack of stored hay, forage, and shelter had starved more than three hundred and fifty thousand head in Montana alone, driving scores of ranchers and speculators into bankruptcy. Keystone hadn't been one of the ranches because Pa'd had the foresight to store enough winter feed to save half of our small herd. About the only good thing in my being locked up in Deer Lodge was that I hadn't had to see and deal with the rotting carcasses strewn across the land, as Pa and hundreds of others had come the '87 spring thaw.

The Keystone marker at the track that angled off the wagon road hung askew now, faded and bullet pocked. The ranch buildings were grouped in a cottonwood-shaded hollow where Little Creek flowed on its winding course to the Yellowstone. My first look at them was painful. Pa had died eight months ago, his health ruined by hard work and shame and the Big Die, and nobody had lived here since. There were gaps in the roofs and wallboards, missing rails in the fences. When Ma was alive there'd been a vegetable garden and even a few flower beds. Nothing now where they'd been except some dried-up vines and weeds, like dug-up bones in a cemetery.

I rode on into the yard, reined in near the house. It would take a hell of a lot of time and effort and no little expense to fix it all up if I decided to stay. And what would I live on meanwhile? Bleak damn prospect, hopeless—

The front door flew open all of a sudden and somebody came running out. The angle of the sun was such that it took a couple of seconds for me to see that it was Mary Beth.

MARY BETH GREATHOUSE

J im!"
I couldn't restrain myself, I rushed straight into his arms as soon as he dismounted and clung to him fiercely. It had been so long since we'd last held each other, so *long*! At first his embrace wasn't as strong as mine, a little tentative, but then his arms tightened and he was holding me with the same intensity. I'd promised myself I wouldn't cry and I didn't, but I had to blink fast and often to keep my eyes dry.

Five years hadn't changed how I felt about him one tiny bit. He was the only man I had ever loved, or could love. And that included the Colonel. My father had been a hard man to feel affection for from my childhood on, and when he tried to drive Jim away from me, then refused my pleas to let me arrange for a good Billings lawyer when Jim was falsely accused, I had quit trying. Now I was nothing more than a dutiful daughter living under his roof, and I wouldn't even be that much longer.

Jim grasped my shoulders finally and held me at arm's length so he could look at me. I wished I had on a dress instead of the buckskin riding habit, that my hair hung long and was combed to a silky dark brown sheen instead of wound up around my head and fastened with shell pins to keep it from tangling in the wind. But it didn't matter, really, because he wasn't examining me in a critical way.

I tried not to examine him that way, either, but he looked so different it made me ache inside. He was leaner than he should be, his face gaunt and missing the rakish mustache he'd sported back in '84, his eyes not as sparkly bright as I remembered them, with none of the devil-may-care boldness that had first attracted me. I reached up to stroke his cheek. When I used to touch him like that, he'd smile and sometimes nuzzle my hand, but he didn't smile now. His expression was grave. He'd shaved recently, but missed a couple of patches and I was shocked to see that the stubble was prematurely flecked with gray.

He said, "I didn't expect to see you so soon, Mary Beth."

"I've been here the past three days, waiting for you. In your last letter you wrote you'd be coming to Keystone, remember?"

"Your father wouldn't like it if he knew."

"But he doesn't. He's been away in Billings on business and he won't be back until tomorrow."

"He must know I'm out, though. And that I'd be coming back. He can't be happy about it."

"No, but there's nothing he can do."

Jim looked away from me for a few moments, into the middle distance, before speaking again. "He's got to know how you feel about me, even if he doesn't know about the letters—the way you've spurned other men the past five years. He's no fool."

"You still feel the same, too, don't you?"

"You know I do."

"Then I don't care what the Colonel thinks. It didn't matter before and it doesn't now."

"He won't stand for us seeing each other again. He'll make things hard for you as well as me."

"He can try. But he won't succeed. We won't let him." I touched his cheek again. "We don't have to stay in Box Elder, be married here," I said. "We can go somewhere far away where nobody knows us, make a new life for ourselves . . ."

"A man's past catches up with him more often than not, one way or another. Besides, I don't much like the idea of being driven from my home a second time, at least not before I have a chance to clear my name."

"Clear your name how?"

"By making Rufus Cable confess."

"My God, Jim, not with violence again—they'll send you back to prison!"

"Don't worry, I won't use my fists on him again." He released my arms. "Where's your horse?"

"In the barn. But I'm not leaving yet, not until we've had a chance to talk a while longer. It's hot out here. Let's go into the house."

He stood without moving or saying anything. I had a

tremendous urge to embrace him again, kiss him long and deep, but I didn't give in to it. It wasn't the right time for that yet.

"Please, Jim."

He shook his head, but he wasn't saying no. It was a bewildered kind of headshake, as if he weren't quite as sure of himself as he sounded. "All right," he said.

He untied his grip and we went to the house. Just inside the door, he stopped and stood looking around at the furnishings, the Indian blanket on the wall, the new braided rug covering part of the puncheon floor. His surprise and his pleasure had a touch of memory sadness mixed in.

"Swept, dusted, aired out, and everything pretty much where I remember it. You do all this, Mary Beth?"

"Yes. The past four days, and on a couple of visits before that."

Jim walked past the horsehair sofa to the pine rocker before the fireplace. The table next to it held his father's rack of pipes and the framed tintype of his mother. He picked up the photograph, looked at it for a time before setting it down and facing me again.

"Ma's china cabinet used to stand against that wall over there," he said. "And there was a bearskin rug under the rocker."

"Gone, along with a few other things. Scavengers. It's a wonder they didn't strip the house bare."

"Doesn't look like they did much damage."

"No, thank God," I said. "I cleaned up what mess there was, here and in the other rooms. Oh, and I brought you two pair of shirts and Levi's—they're in the bedroom."

He smiled then for the first time. "Homecoming presents," he said. "Three of them."

"Three? Just the cleanup and the clothes—"

"You're forgetting the most important. You."

He took me into his arms again, and I clung to him as tightly as before. He was filled with confused and conflicted feelings, yes, but not about me. That was what mattered, that he loved and wanted me as much as I loved and wanted him. From now on, neither the Colonel nor anyone else was going to keep us apart.

WILL SATTERLEE

It was late afternoon when Seth Jennison finally got around to informing me that Jim Tarbeaux had returned. I chided him for not letting me know immediately so I could have buttonholed Tarbeaux before he arranged transportation with Sam Benson for passage out to his ranch. Still, it was not too late to interview him for tomorrow's issue of the *Banner*. Keystone was only a little over seven miles from town, a tolerable round-trip drive.

I left the office immediately and walked the four blocks to the house R.W. and I shared. I often walk to and from work when weather permits, even on hot summer days such as this one. Dr. Phillips says the exercise is good for my heart, which has a slight murmur, and also helps keep my blood pressure at a manageable level.

I hitched up our buggy, raised the hood to protect myself from the sun, and drove out to Keystone. Even though the day had cooled some, I was perspiring heavily when I neared the ranch. As I came around the last turn in the dusty wagon road, a lone rider emerged from the Keystone track and cantered off across the prairie. The horse was an Appaloosa, the rider a woman—Mary Beth Great-house. She had wasted no time renewing her acquaintance with Jim Tarbeaux.

I had not been out to Keystone since George Tar-beaux passed on, and as I expected, the compound had suffered noticeably from its eight months' neglect. The ranch had never been a showplace, but George had kept it up to the best of his ability after Jim was sent to prison, even after the devastating winter that had cost him half of his small herd. I wondered what Jim's reaction to its deteriorating state had been when he rode in today.

He came striding from the barn when he heard my buggy rattle into the yard, stopped nearby and stood with his hands on his hips as I set the brake and climbed down. "Mr. Satterlee," he said by way of greeting, making half a question of my name.

Without being obvious about it, I studied him as we shook hands. Prison had changed him, but perhaps for the better. The last time I had seen him, he was a callow, reckless youth; now he was a man. There was hardness in him, reflected in his eyes and the set of his jaw, but it struck me as the hardness of maturity, not the cold, bitter meanness that prison instills in some men.

"I heard you were back, Jim. I've come to tell you how sorry I am about your father's passing—"

"So am I. More than I can say."

"—and to welcome you home."

"You'll be one of the few," he said without apparent rancor. "I reckon I'm still a pariah in most folks' eyes."

"Not mine. I haven't changed my mind about your innocence. An opinion I have stated in the *Banner* and intend to continue stating."

"I appreciate that." He said the words through a humorless half-smile, but the expression of gratitude seemed sincere.

My face was streaming sweat; I dried it with my handkerchief, fanned my face with my hat.

"Hot out here in the sun," he said. "You're welcome in the house."

"Thank you, but I won't stay long. Mind if I ask what you're planning to do, Jim?"

"About what? The ranch? Rufus Cable?"

"Both."

"I haven't decided yet." He waved a hand that encompassed the rundown property. "Take a lot of time and money to fix the place up. Money I don't have, no matter what most folks think. All I've got is what I came out of Deer Lodge with and that won't last long. And nobody is likely to give me the kind of loan I'd need."

"Selling is always an option," I said.

"Who'd buy it, land and beef prices being what they are?"

"Someone not interested in cattle ranching might."

"Nesters? No, I wouldn't sell to one of them. Not after

all the work Pa put into this ranch. Ma, too, before she died. And my contribution before Cable gouged five years out of my life."

"You haven't seen him yet, have you?"

"No."

"But you plan to."

"Eventually."

"And when you do?"

He showed the mirthless smile again. "I'd like nothing better than to clear my name and make him pay for what he did to me, but I won't resort to violence to do it. The last thing I want is to spend even one more minute behind bars."

I believed him. "Well, then, I'll make that clear in my editorial in tomorrow's edition of the *Banner.*"

"Obliged for that, too."

I would have liked to ask him about Mary Beth, what his intentions were, but I had the feeling he would close up on me if I did. I was not supposed to know about the letters they had exchanged—no one was. It was only by accident that I had learned about them from Etta Lohrman, and I had sworn to her that I would not betray the confidence. Tarbeaux would have been perfectly within his rights to tell me his relationship with Mary Beth was none of my business. We had established a rapport; it would have been a mistake on my part to jeopardize it.

We shook hands again and I climbed back into the

buggy. "If there is anything else I can do for you," I said then, "don't hesitate to ask."

"I appreciate that, but I won't be asking favors. Whatever I do, I'll do it on my own."

"Good luck to you, then."

He nodded. "I'll need it, Mr. Satterlee."

"Will," I said. "My friends call me Will."

NED FOLEY

I have been tending bar at Occidental House for nigh on ten years now, the Occidental being Box Elder's premier watering hole and gambling parlor. It has ruby-glass chandeliers, a polished Brunswicke bar backed by gilt-edged mirrors, red satin wall hangings, the best free lunch in town (pickled herring our specialty), and a side room through an archway where customers can play stud or draw poker, or buck the tiger or bet on the red, black, and double O. No percentage girls per se, though we do have what Tate Reynolds, the Occidental's owner, calls "hostesses" who are of a better class than most.

Our clientele is mostly townsmen, cattlemen, drummers and other travelers passing through. But Tate's a democratic gent; anybody who has the price of a drink and doesn't cause trouble is welcome. Nesters don't come in much, just now and then for a beer or two and usually in small bunches. They keep pretty much to themselves, same as the ranchers and cowhands. Every so often a remark will get passed between the two factions, but there's yet to be any fighting on the premises. But it's an uneasy truce, here and everywhere else in the basin. So far cooler heads than Colonel Elijah Greathouse's have prevailed. For how long is anybody's guess.

Most days and nights in the Occidental pass without incident. Oh, now and then somebody will take too much liquor and cause a ruckus, especially after the spring and fall roundups when cowhands come in to let off steam and blow some or all of their pay, but not nearly as many as before the Great Die-Up. Skirmishes are few and far between, and sidearms not being allowed within the town limits, there hasn't been a single incidence of gunplay in my ten years behind the bar. One set of fisticuffs we had was downright amusing, and it didn't involve locals. A couple of patent-medicine drummers got into an argument one afternoon over which of them sold the best cure-all for a variety of ills and afflictions and would have beat each other unconscious if I hadn't put an end to it with my bung-starter. The amusing part was, we found out afterward that both patent medicines were manufactured by the same company in Chicago and neither of those pecker-woods knew it.

There hadn't been a whisper of trouble in over two months when Elrod Patch came in Wednesday night at a few minutes past ten. Uh-oh, I thought when I spotted him. He couldn't have picked a worse night.

Usually Patch does his drinking in the Ace High and the other cheap saloons over in Shantyville, but every now and then he'll wander into the Occidental. He's tolerable if more or less sober, but when he's carrying a load he can be more obnoxious and contentious than usual if anybody so much as looks at him cross-eyed. He was carrying one tonight, judging by his slight stagger as he crossed the room. He was alone, naturally. If Patch had any friends or drinking companions in or around Box Elder, I had never heard of them.

What made the situation problematical was the fact that one of the other customers was Berne Rheinmiller, the young son of a German farmer out on Big Creek. He wasn't a regular, either; in fact, this was only about the third time I'd seen him, the other two times being when he'd come into town late in the day for supplies. Tonight, though, he'd been here for over an hour nibbling on schnapps with a Norwegian his age named Harald something. He was building up a load of his own—I was about ready to cut him off—and angrily telling anyone who'd listen how Patch had cheated his old man on a deal they'd made for a new plowshare. There wasn't any question that the story was true. Patch didn't like nesters any more than Colonel Greathouse did.

The Rheinmiller youngster didn't see him at first; he was at the far end of the bar, his back turned, talking to Harald. There was plenty of room at the bar—we weren't all that busy, it being a weeknight—and Patch bellied up near where I was and snapped out an order for beer. That eased my fears some, though not much. As long as he wasn't drinking whiskey punches, he was a mite easier to get along with.

I poured him a mug and slid it along the bar. The men on either side weren't crowding him, but they each moved a foot or two anyway to make sure he had plenty of elbow room. One of them, George Petrie, a clerk in the freight office, said something to him, polite. The glare George got in return closed his mouth, decided him to hurry up and swallow the rest of his drink and walk on out.

Petrie's place was taken by the new printer at the *Banner,* Artemas Jones. He'd bought a beer and introduced himself when he first came in. Affable gent, more so than most rolling stones. It was unusual for one of his breed to patronize the Occidental, their drinking and gambling being pretty much confined to the same Shantyville saloons Patch frequented, but this fellow had money in his pocket—poker winnings from the last place he'd worked, he said. He'd been playing stud at Pete Ryan's table in the gaming room the past couple of hours, looking to fatten his stake.

"Another beer?" I asked him.

"One for the road."

I kept one eye on Patch as I drew it. His glass was mostly empty and he was squinting at himself in the mirror, his head haloed in smoke from one of the three-for-a-nickel stogies he favored. The smell of it was as potent awful as Indian kinnikinnick, strong enough to overpower the combined odors of better tobacco, beer, sawdust, sweat, and the hostesses' perfume.

"How'd you make out?" I asked Jones when I served him.

"Lost most of what I had. Thirty-two dollars."

"Too bad."

He shrugged and said philosophically, "Easy come, easy go."

Patch guzzled the last of his brew, licked foam off his mustache, and called for a refill. In a loud voice, this time.

And that was when the trouble started.

Berne Rheinmiller turned around at the sound of Patch's voice, peered his way, then smacked his empty glass down on the bar and came stomping over. His first mistake was laying a hand on Patch's shoulder and pulling him around. His second was half shouting, "You damned crook!"

It got quiet in there all of a sudden, real quiet. Seemed like everybody froze, too, as if like Lot's wife they'd all been turned into pillars of salt. The only one who moved was me. I started edging over to where I kept my bungstarter handy under the bar.

Patch jerked the kid's hand off, glowered blearily at him. "Who you callin' a crook?"

"You cheated Hugo Rheinmiller yesterday, shamed him."

"I never cheated nobody."

"Four dollars extra you tried to charge for the plow-share, then you stole a dollar from him—"

"Stole! Like hell I did."

I said, "Take it easy, gents, no trouble now," but neither of them paid any attention to me.

"Who the hell are you, kid?" Patch said. "Kin to that Heinie out at Little Creek?"

"Berne Rheinmiller, son of Hugo."

"Son of a bitch is more like it, calling me a crook."

That provoked Rheinmiller into making his third mistake. He lunged and swung at Patch. Patch stayed the blow by catching the youngster's fist in a huge paw, then shoved him backward into one of the tables. The momentum from the shove twisted Patch into the printer, Jones, who was standing there next to him mug in hand. Beer and foam splattered all over the front of Jones's sack coat.

He said, "Hey!" and threw his shoulder into Patch—a reflex action, the way it looked. The blacksmith staggered, grunted, and without looking at Jones, swung a beefy arm sideways into his chest and knocked him down onto the brass foot rail. When he landed, I heard one of the spittoons go clanging across the floor. Then Patch let out a bellow and went after Rheinmiller.

It was no contest. The youngster was shaken up from his collision with the table and his coordination was none too good anyway from the schnapps. Patch caught hold of him with one paw and hit him three or four times with the other in quick succession, then picked him up squirming and hollering. He was in such a rage by then that he pulled Rheinmiller into a horizontal stretch across the front of his body, then brought his knee up as if he were getting ready to slam the kid down across it. If he'd done that, bull-strong as he was, he'd likely have broken Rheinmiller's back.

I vaulted over the bar with my bungstarter, but I banged my knee and it slowed me down. Everybody else was too afraid of Patch to make a move to stop him, all except Jones, who'd hauled himself off the floor still clutching his empty mug. He got there before I did, and just in the nick of time. The Occidental's mugs are heavy cut glass and the roundhouse swing he made with it slammed into the side of Patch's head with a sound like a hammer hitting a melon. Patch went down in a heap, Rheinmiller on top of him.

Harald and a couple of others moved then, untangled the youngster, dazed and bloody, and lifted him and sat him down in a chair. Patch didn't move, didn't make a sound. His eyes were open, rolled up with most of the whites showing. There was blood on his mouth and a piece of something yellow-black glinting on his chin. The blow must have broken off one of his snaggle teeth.

Jones said, "He's not dead, I hope."

I knelt down to check the pulse in Patch's neck. "Cold-cocked, that's all. Good thing you didn't hit him any harder."

Somebody said, "Well, that's open to debate," and there wasn't any disagreement.

Jones and I and two others picked Patch up, carried him out into the alley in back, and laid him on a patch of grass under a half-dead cottonwood. When we came back inside, Harald had taken Rheinmiller away—to Dr. Phillips for treatment, probably. Several customers, myself included, offered to treat Jones to beer and he accepted twice before he called it a night.

"Who is Patch anyway?" he asked me when I brought him the first.

"Local blacksmith."

"Doesn't seem to be much liked."

"He isn't. Mean and spiteful, if not exactly crooked. You did the right thing hitting him the way you did, saved that youngster from being hurt worse than he is. But there's something you need to know about Elrod Patch."

"What's that?"

"He's a grudge holder," I said. "Were I you, I'd be real careful to avoid him the rest of your stay in Box Elder."

R. W. SATTERLEE

Printing day was always a chore. The work was long and hard, especially when there was just two of us to get it all done and the week's edition out on schedule. Part of my job was to feed the ink roller, so I went in to the office ahead of Dad. Give-a-Damn Jones was already there, resetting a portion of Dad's editorial, the part dealing with Jim Tarbeaux's return yesterday, that Dad had written last night.

"Were you able to get a room at the Travelers' Rest?" I asked him.

"I was. Better lodgings than some I've had."

"What about your horse? Did you sell it?"

"The livery owner bought it for a pittance," Artemas said. "He didn't want the saddle, though. Neither did the saddle maker, Rufus Cable. You wouldn't happen to know anyone interested in buying one, would you?"

"I wish I did, but I don't. I could ask around."

"Don't put yourself out, R.W. The saddle's not worth much."

"What'd you do with it? Take it to the Travelers' Rest?"

"No. Mr. Benson let me leave it at the livery. Maybe I can talk him into paying me a dollar for it before I leave."

I set to work with the ink. Artemas finished the resetting, ran off a galley of the front page for a final check. Pretty soon he said, "Your father's editorial is pretty strong stuff." He ran an ink-creased finger over the dual headlines: **Box Elder's Little Napoleon** and below it in smaller type, **A Miscarriage of Justice.** "He really does have it in for Colonel Greathouse."

"Yes, he does."

"This is sure to infuriate the rancher."

"I know. But Dad's not afraid of him. Or afraid to speak his mind when he feels wrongs have been done and folks like the settlers and Jim Tarbeaux mistreated."

"He's outspoken in his defense of Tarbeaux, but he doesn't say why he thinks the man was wrongly convicted."

"He can't on account of the libel laws," I said. "He's one of the few who believes it. Most folks think Tarbeaux hid or buried the money somewhere and that he's come back to fetch it. The editorial probably won't change their minds."

"Who does your father think stole the money?"

"Rufus Cable. He's the only one who could have. He was a hotel clerk at the time and for about a year afterward. Dad figures he bought the saddle shop with part of the stolen cash, but he couldn't prove it and neither could anybody else. He—"

Dad came in just then and I shut up quick. He tended to be grumpy and short-tempered on press days. This Thursday he was already scowling and snappy when he passed through the rail divider into the press room.

He looked at Artemas and demanded, "What's this I hear about an altercation between you and Elrod Patch in the Occidental last night?"

"It wasn't exactly an altercation, Mr. Satterlee."

"No? I was told you knocked him cold with a beer mug."

"Guilty as charged."

"I take a dim view of my employees brawling in public, Jones."

"I don't make a habit of it. And I had cause."

"I was told that, too."

"Seemed like the right thing to do at the time."

"Yes, evidently you were justified," Dad admitted. "Saved young Rheinmiller from a beating or worse."

This was all news to me and it had me wide-eyed. I wanted to ask Artemas why he hadn't mentioned the incident to me, but maybe he wasn't one to brag. Instead I asked, "Was Patch hurt bad?"

"No. He was seen in his smithy this morning."

In a way that was a shame, Patch being a lout and a bully. But I knew Dad wouldn't have liked me saying so, so I kept still. I vowed to ask Artemas when we were alone together again just what had happened last night. Any man who would stand up to Elrod Patch was a hero in my view.

"Do you intend to write an account of the incident, Mr. Satterlee?"

"It is my duty to report the news."

"Yes, sir," Artemas said, "but it's not much of a story. The layouts for this issue are all complete—we'd have to drop column inches and reset."

"And it would just make Patch madder than he already is," I blurted.

Dad narrowed his eyes at me. But he gave it some thought and then allowed that I was right. "There is nothing to be gained in provoking the man," he said. "A brief mention in next week's issue will suffice."

I went on spreading ink with a palette knife, moving the roller through it until it was full, then taking the roller to the press to ink the forms once Dad tightened down the quoins. It wouldn't have been as difficult a job if the roller hadn't been so worn at one end that we kept getting monks on the outside columns. Each time I had to reink and Dad had to fix a fresh sheet of paper to the marks in the tympan, snap the tympan down, and roll the form under the platen for another try. The monks got him so frustrated he started pulling harder than necessary on the elbow-shaped chill that slammed the platen down on the bed. Then when he let go of the lever and the platen jumped back up again, he had to roll the bed out, lift the printed sheet off the form, toss it aside, and replace it with another.

Give-a-Damn Jones being there made the work easier than when it was just Dad and me. He had all the page forms finished and ready, except for having to reset part of the editorial. But setting type wasn't all he did this day. Some typographers won't do anything but set type; Jones wasn't one of them. He helped wet down the newsprint in preparation for the run, carried the heavy finished forms to the Albion, showed Dad and me a little trick that helped get rid of the monks, and made a couple of adjustments on the old press that soon had it operating more smoothly than normal.

We finished the press run early as a result. The four sheets looked fine, very clean for a change, with no typos or misplaced lines. Dad lost some of his grumpiness and allowed as how he was satisfied, an admission he seldom made and that for him amounted to high praise.

I had the papers bundled and ready when the delivery boys, Spence and Pete Donovan, came in to pick them up. We closed shop and Dad and I went over to the Elite Café for a late, light midday meal. I invited Artemas to join us, but he begged off, saying he had some business to attend to. He winked at me as he said it—Dad's back was turned. A kind of man-to-man wink that I took to mean his "business" involved a visit to Tillie Johnson's parlor house behind the Free and Easy Saloon—a place I wasn't supposed to know about but had since I was about twelve.

"In the *daytime*?" I blurted.

He laughed. "No law against it."

"No law against what?" Dad asked.

I couldn't think of an answer and I felt my face getting

warm. Artemas saved me by saying, "Against a man wetting his whistle after a hard day's work."

"I suppose not." Dad wasn't a teetotaler, but he didn't believe in drinking alcohol of any kind until after nightfall. Or indulging in any other pleasures, likely, though he'd never spoken of such matters.

I hid an embarrassed smile as I watched Artemas walk off toward the railroad depot. Dad would have been furious if he knew that I was more than a little envious of where I figured Give-a-Damn Jones was bound.

COLONEL ELIJAH
GREATHOUSE

Mary Beth was saddling Southwind, her leopard-spotted Appaloosa, when I came into the stable. She was dressed in her riding habit, but she had on that silly little porkpie hat she favored instead of the Stetson she usually wore, and her hair was combed down long instead of braided and rolled.

"Where you off to, girl?"

"Just out for a ride. All my chores are done."

"Gone how long?"

"I don't know, a while. I may go into town."

"Stay away from Jim Tarbeaux," I said.

She turned as I spoke so I couldn't see her face. Without saying anything, she slung her sidesaddle onto Southwind's back, easy as a man would, and began cinching it tight.

"You heard me, Mary Beth. Stay away from him."

"What makes you think Jim's come back?"

"One of the hands saw him in town yesterday. Kinch told me when I came home last night."

"I'm of age, Father. You can't tell me what to do or whom I can see anymore."

"I can, by God, as long as you're still living under my roof."

"Well, maybe I won't be much longer."

I could feel my spine stiffen. "That better not mean you're thinking of running off with him."

"You can't stop me if I do."

"The devil I can't. He's a no-account thief, an ex-convict—"

Mary Beth said in that half angry, half snotty way she had when she was defending Tarbeaux to me, "I'll say it again for the hundredth time—he didn't steal Tom Kendall's money."

"It doesn't matter whether he did or not. He's still a jailbird. No daughter of mine is going to shame me by taking up with a jailbird!"

"Shame *you*. That's your real objection, isn't it? Not that people will think badly of me, but that they'll think worse of you than they already do."

"You watch your mouth, girl!"

She didn't say anything else. Just backed Southwind out of his stall, took hold of the reins and swung up to curl her leg around the saddle horn, then rode past me up the runway. Mad as I was, I couldn't help feeling a cut of pride at the way she sat and rode, straight and easy and surehanded. Not like Gloria, God rest her soul, who hadn't cared for riding horseback and was clumsy whenever I talked her into it. Like a man born to the saddle. Like a soldier.

Her mother had tried to make a pure lady out of her, and so had I for a time after Gloria died. She flat-out refused when I tried to send her back East for a year or two at one of those ladies' finishing schools. Too high-spirited for her own good. Spent most of her time honing her tomboy tendencies—riding, roping, riding fence and helping with the branding, rifle shooting with a fair amount of accuracy. Well, if I couldn't have the son I'd wanted for my heir, at least Mary Beth and whoever she married would be capable of running the Square G when I went to my reward. If she ever married. The girl had a doltish streak when it came to men, taking up with wrong ones like Tarbeaux and turning up her nose at the right ones who came courting.

I watched her ride out of the ranch yard. On her way to see him, for sure. And for sure I was not about to let her throw her life away on that goddamned good-for-nothing jailbird. I hadn't liked the cut of him when he'd been sparking her before the robbery; a wild and worthless range bum in the making. He hadn't been good enough for Mary Beth then, and he sure as hell wasn't good enough for her now. I'd put a stop to the fool romance then and I'd put a stop to it again now.

One more aggravation in a week's worth. The trip to Billings had been a waste of time, left a sour taste in my mouth. The goddamned bank had refused for the third time now to give me a loan, and the goddamned Prairie Cattle Company refused to increase the number of steers they were willing to buy this fall, mine and those owned by the other local ranchers in the Association, or to raise their price per head. Same old excuse—times were still hard, the beef industry in such a severe decline it likely would never recover. The glory days of open-range cattle ranching were a thing of the past, they said, finished off by the Great Die-Up. Bullshit. But they just wouldn't listen.

And as if those turndowns weren't enough, Frank Wickwire had failed to use his lawyer's wiles to convince the Territorial Legislature to put a moratorium on the deeding off of any more rangeland to the goddamned sod-busters. Montana was due for statehood next year and settlement was being encouraged now instead of the other way around. That was *their* excuse.

I went into the house, into my study, and futzed around with tally sheets and other paperwork for a while, but I was too damned restless and upset to concentrate. I wanted to have a talk with Jada Kinch, but he was out mending fence with a couple of the other hands and wouldn't be back until late afternoon. I poured myself a large whiskey and went out onto the porch and stood surveying my property.

The compound was on high ground, backed and shaded by cottonwoods and a couple of big box elders, the main house higher than the rest so I had a broad view of the hip-roofed barn, the two bunkhouses, the cookhouse and smokehouse, the clumps of buffalo berry and chokecherry that lined Big Creek, the bunch-grass prairie that stretched out beyond the whitewashed fences, the Knob in one direction and the glint of the Yellowstone in the other. When I came out here to settle at the end of the war, the prairie had been black with buffalo. They were mostly gone now, killed off by hide hunters and parties of Easterners and Englishmen hunting for sport. Gone same as the vast herds of cattle that roamed the open prairie land before the Great Die-Up.

It had taken me nearly twenty years to build the Square G into the biggest, most productive cattle ranch in this basin. I had had to step on a few that got in my way, as well as fight off Sioux raiding parties before and after that fool Custer got himself and his troops slaughtered at Little Big Horn, and hunt down and hang rustlers white and red, but that was the kind of hard country it was those days—survival of the fittest.

Then that goddamned disastrous winter. Should've seen it coming. Should've paid attention to what the reservation Blackfeet and Crow were saying, the preparations they were making. And to the summer being so hot and dry that range fires kept breaking out in the shriveled grass. And to the bark on the young cottonwoods thicker than ever before in the fall, birds bunching earlier than usual, heavy coats on the wild animals.

All the signs were there, but I'd been too busy to see them and take the necessary precautions to protect my herd, what with the goddamned greedy speculators shipping cattle in from all directions, overland and on every westbound train. Texas longhorns, Durhams, mixed-blood shorthorns from Missouri, Canadian beef, breeding stock and pilgrim steers from the Midwest . . . thousands grazing everywhere you looked that summer and fall, encroaching on my land, intermingling with my stock. At the last fall roundup tally before the blizzards came, more than six thousand head of blooded native beef had carried the Square G brand and I employed a permanent crew of twelve and several more for each roundup. Now the tally ran to less than fourteen hundred head at the spring roundup, a third of those no longer pure, and I had a permanent crew of five and couldn't afford but a handful of loose riders in the spring and fall.

It used to be that viewing my holdings from here and from out on the range gave me a feeling of pride and satisfaction, the same feeling I'd had when I surveyed the troops under my command before the Franklin-Nashville Campaign and our pursuit of Hood and what was left of his division to the Tennessee River at the tag end of the war. But not any more. These days the vista made me feel bitter and angry. It just wasn't the same anymore. The mass buffalo slaughter, the Great Die-Up, the sodbusters with their plows and barbed-wire fences, the sons of bitches in Billings and Great Falls and Helena . . . change, progress, statehood . . . all combining to rob me of what was rightfully mine and tarnish my view of what was left.

But that wasn't all there was to stick heavy in my craw today. Oh, hell, no. One of the cook's helpers came back from town with a wagonload of supplies and a copy of the latest issue of the *Box Elder Banner*. And there smack on the front page was another of Satterlee's goddamned editorials, this one an even greater outrage than the ones he'd written before. **Box Elder's Little Napoleon.** Christ! A petty tyrant, he called me, a scourge, a blot, a danger to the welfare of the valley's future prosperity on account of "his relentless crusade against change and growth and the rolling wheels of progress."

It made me so crazy mad I couldn't see straight. I tore the paper into shreds, threw them on the ground, stomped them into dust with my boots. And then I stalked to the barn to saddle my claybank. A man can only take so much crap, and I'd had my fill of Satterlee's and then some.

He would pay for this repeated soiling of my good name, just as Tarbeaux would pay for trying to soil Mary Beth's. One way or another, by God. One way or another.

RUFUS CABLE

Jim Tarbeaux was back. Came in on the noon train yesterday, rented a horse and headed out to what's left of Keystone ranch. Word gets around fast in Box Elder—it hadn't taken long for it to come to me, from the first man I encountered when I left the shop last evening.

Why hadn't Tarbeaux come straight to me? He must've walked right past the shop on his way to the livery. Unarmed yet, maybe. Or just making me sweat some more. I tried to tell myself five years behind bars might have changed his mind about carrying out his threat, but I didn't believe it. He wasn't the kind to stop hating. If anything, prison had made a hard case out of him and even more determined. Sooner or later he'd keep his vow.

No matter how hard I tried, I couldn't stop thinking about the spring of '83. It was all as vivid in my memory as if it had happened five days instead of five years ago.

Twenty years old that spring, me and Tarbeaux both. Knew each other because we'd gone to school together, grown up together, but we weren't friends. I was a town kid, he was a rancher's son. Too little in common. Too much free spirit in him and none in me—I knew it about myself even then. He went places and did things I was too timid to even consider.

After he turned eighteen he'd started hanging out with Bob Kendall, who lived on Anchor a few miles from George Tarbeaux's Keystone. The reckless streak in him widened out over the next two years, as did an even more irresponsible streak of wildness in Bob Kendall. Drinking, gambling, whoring. Neither of them had gotten into serious trouble, just enough to make Marshal Jennison pay some mind to them.

No one paid much mind to me, meanwhile. Quiet and steady, that was the best anybody had to say about Rufus Cable. Quiet, steady—and honest. Saddle-making and leatherwork were what I craved to do with my life. Vernon Norris, the only saddle maker in town, had let me help in his shop for pocket change, but he was too cheap to hire me as a full-time apprentice. I would have moved to another town, Billings or Miles City, except that Ma's arthritis got so bad she could no longer do seamstress work, and she was too old and set in her ways to want to live out her days anywhere but Box Elder. All up to me then to take care of her, put food on the table. And the only job I could find that paid a decent wage was night clerk at the Box Elder Hotel.

Ma died sudden in March of that year. And I was alone and miserable, facing a future as bleak as a Montana winter, until that day in late April when the chance of a life-time, a temptation impossible to resist, came my way.

Tarbeaux and Bob Kendall had led the drive of a combined herd of Anchor and Keystone cattle to Miles City for sale to the Prairie Cattle Company. George Tarbeaux's share of the tally had been paid by bank draft, but Tom Kendall didn't trust banks and had insisted on cash. Five thousand four hundred dollars. Bob was supposed to come back right away and deliver the money to his father, but he had a woman in Miles City and was hell-bent on a few days of fun. Tarbeaux wanted to remain in Miles as well, to blow off some steam of his own, as he put it, but Bob paid him twenty-five dollars to return to Box Elder and make the delivery in his stead.

It was after dark when Tarbeaux got back. He was tired and didn't feel like riding all the way out to Anchor and then home to Keystone, so he rented a room from me at the hotel for the night. A few minutes after he went upstairs, he came back down with the money belt he'd been wearing loosely rolled up under his coat. The lobby was empty when he laid it on the counter and said, "Rufus, put this in the hotel safe for tonight. I'll fetch it first thing in the morning." But he didn't think to ask for a claim check.

He went out to the café for a quick meal, then up to the saloons in Shantyville to drink and gamble. It was three hours later by the hotel clock when he returned, half drunk.

Burning curiosity made me open the money belt in the privacy of the hotel office after Tarbeaux staggered up to bed. The sight of all those greenbacks weakened my knees, dried my mouth. I put the belt back in the safe, but I couldn't stop thinking about it. A boldness, a recklessness built in me for the first time as the hours passed and the money became an obsession. I might have been able to overcome it if Ma had still been alive, but with her gone and me on my own and miserable, I couldn't stop myself. Just couldn't stop myself.

I took the bag from the safe an hour past midnight, carried it out back of the hotel stables and hid it in a clump of greasewood. Afterward I barely remembered doing it, as if it had all happened in a dream.

Tarbeaux came down early in the morning, just as the day clerk arrived to relieve me. There was a storm inside me, but the money was all I let myself think about when I faced him. The money, the money, the money! Outwardly I was calm and the lies came easier than I imagined they would. Money belt? I didn't know anything about it. I had been given nothing to put in the safe the night before.

The disbelief in his eyes turned to hate and then blind rage. The ruckus he raised brought several people running, all witnesses to his violent attack on me. I was bawling from the pain of half a dozen blows when Marshal Jennison and two others pulled him off me and took him to jail.

My word against Tarbeaux's, my quiet, honest reputation against his wild one. The marshal believed me, the

Kendalls believed me, the townspeople believed me. At the trial, the county prosecutor accused Tarbeaux of attempting to frame me for the crime, instead of the other way around. And of hiding most of the money and gambling away the rest in the Shantyville saloons—he'd been bucking the tiger and losing that night, though no one at the Free and Easy could say for sure how much. The fact that he'd claimed to be too tired to ride to Anchor and checked into the hotel instead, yet then went and spent three hours gambling and drinking, weighed heavily against him. As did his unprovoked assault on me. As did my solemn and unswerving testimony. The jury didn't believe his claim that he'd gone to the Free and Easy for just one drink and had the poor judgment to have several more while he played and lost at faro. They didn't believe he'd given me the money belt to put in the hotel safe. They believed me.

The only ones who didn't were Will Satterlee and Mary Beth Greathouse. Satterlee, damn him, wrote editorials implying I was the thief—was still writing them. But they hadn't mattered then and they didn't matter now.

I still remember the pain of the beating Tarbeaux inflicted on me. And I still hear his vow of vengeance as he was being led from the courtroom. "You won't get away with this, Cable! You'll pay for it. As soon as I get out I'll come back and nail your hide to a barn wall!"

The threat shook me some at the time. But five years seemed like a long way off then and it hadn't bothered me for long. Neither had my conscience. I had the money, re-buried now in a safe place near the river outside of town, and I had my plans. Not spending any of those greenbacks right away wasn't easy, but I made myself wait because Vernon Norris's health was poor and I knew he was getting ready to sell his shop and move to Bozeman to live with his son. And when that day came, his saddle shop was mine.

For the last four years I worked hard and lived well, despite losing the rest of the money on a bad investment. Mostly I didn't think about Tarbeaux; I had too many other things on my mind, the worst of them the consumption and the doctors' diagnosis. It wasn't until one day a few weeks ago that I realized how soon he would be released. Then and all the days since I was consumed by a different worry, a different fear.

Should I keep waiting for him to come to me, or take the bull by the horns and force the showdown? Either way, the confrontation and its outcome scared me spitless. But I couldn't go on like this much longer. I hadn't slept more than a couple of hours any of the past few nights, kept waking up soaked in sweat whenever I did doze off. It had to end soon or I'd come apart at the seams like a cheap Mexican saddle.

WILL SATTERLEE

It is my custom to keep the *Banner* office open until six o'clock on Thursdays, so I had returned after my mid-afternoon meal with R.W. and was at my desk attending to paperwork when the front door flew open and Colonel Elijah Greathouse stormed in. He slammed the door hard enough to rattle the glass, stepped up to the counter and stood glaring at me across it. When I didn't rise immediately from my desk, he banged one of his large fists on the countertop.

"Satterlee! Come over here and face me!"

I remained seated. "This is my shop, Colonel. I take orders from no one and I expect civility from visitors."

"Civility, my arse." On the counter was a stack of the current issue of the *Banner;* he snatched one up, held it at arm's length, and stabbed a blunt forefinger into my editorial forcefully enough to tear a hole in the newsprint. "You'll get none from me after this outrage."

"Five cents," I said.

". . . What?"

"For the issue in your hand. You damaged it, you'll pay for it."

"Like hell I will!"

I stood slowly and went through the division gate to stand in front of him. He was a sight as always in his habitual range outfit of buckskin jacket, Union Army tunic, and stagged pants stuffed into scuffed black boots. His shoulder-length graying hair hung in sweaty curls from beneath his Stetson; his untrimmed soup-strainer mustache was caked with dust. Spots of foamy lather marbled his pantlegs, I noticed, testimony to how hard and how carelessly he had ridden his horse from the Square G. Anyone who had never seen him before might take him for an old-style buffalo hunter or a hardscrabble rancher, not the still-powerful leader of the Cattlemen's Association he fancied himself to be. I restrained myself from telling him so.

"'Box Elder's Little Napoleon.' Libel, by God!"

"No it isn't. It is a statement of fact. As is everything else I wrote."

"The devil it is. All that horseshit about my being a scourge and a danger to the welfare of the community. Bringing up those lies about my war record again. Claiming that thief Tarbeaux was railroaded—"

"I never said he was railroaded. Only that I believe him to have been the victim of a miscarriage of justice."

"—and implying I'll raise hell with him if he tries to stay on at Keystone. It's goddamned outrageous, all of it!"

"Freedom of the press, Colonel. And I will thank you not to use profanity when speaking to me."

"I'll say anything I goddamned well please, same as you." So great was his indignant anger that his mustaches quivered. No . . . that bright, hard glint in his eyes was more than just anger, it was the shine of incipient dementia. The man truly was losing his grip. "I demand a retraction, or by God you'll suffer the consequences."

"I don't respond to threats."

"You'd better respond to this one. Will you issue a retraction?"

"I will not."

"All right then, editor. But hear this and hear it good. Write one more vicious lie about me and I'll see to it you pay and pay dear, in one type of coin or another."

"I defy you to make that statement in front of witnesses."

"You think I'm just talking through my hat? Keep prodding me, you'll find out."

"Just what will you do if I continue to tell the truth about you and your high-handed ways? Have me beaten up? Damage my property as you've done to the immigrant farmers'?"

"More lies. I've done no such thing."

"Have me shot from ambush some dark night?"

He banged his fist on the counter again. "Damn you, Satterlee, I'm no killer."

"No? Your past record tells a different tale."

"What past record? There were few casualties in the

campaigns I led during the war, and none that weren't justified on the field of combat."

"Can you say the same about the men you shot or hung the past twenty years?"

"Men! Rustlers, renegade Indians, riffraff. I had every right to protect my property."

"According to your dubious code of conduct."

"Those were lawless times and you know it. You'd have done the same as me and a hundred others if you'd been around then and threatened as we were."

"I doubt that. I am a peaceable man."

"A weak man, you mean," Greathouse said with a sneer in his voice. "A goddamned ink-stained agitator hiding behind the First Amendment."

I pride myself on my self-control, but I can be pushed just so far before anger flares in me, too, and I respond in kind. Greathouse has the knack of prodding me to that point far more quickly than any other individual I have ever known.

"And you, Colonel," I said, "are a knave, a blowhard, and a fool. Get off my property immediately or I'll summon the marshal and have you arrested for harassment. And don't set foot in here again, ever, under any circumstances."

We stood matching stares for several seconds. Then he muttered something obscene, turned and opened the door. I called after him, "You still owe me a nickel for the paper," but he ignored the parting shot, stepped through, and again slammed the door behind him.

JADA KINCH

An hour or so after Miss Mary Beth left the Square G on Friday, Colonel Greathouse sent me and Al Yandle over to the Keystone ranch. He figured that was where she'd been going the past few days, not out riding alone like she said but over there to see Tarbeaux.

The Colonel had been on the prod since he got back from Billings, Will Satterlee's latest horseshit editorial festering in him like a boil. I'd been with him twelve years now, through good times and bad, and him and me don't always see eye to eye. More'n once I've been tempted to draw my pay and hit the trail. But at thirty-seven I'm too old now to become a loose rider; I'll be ramrodding for the Colonel until one or the other of us drops dead, and he knows it as well as I do. Besides which, when it comes to Satterlee, and Tarbeaux and Miss Mary Beth, we do see eye to eye. I felt as riled as he did and for the same reasons. Seemed like nothing went right for him or the Square G any more, and when it don't go right for them, it don't go right for me.

There was a rise rimmed with cottonwoods a couple of hundred rods west of the Keystone ranch buildings. Me and Yandle rode up into the trees from the blind side, picketed our horses, and went to where we had a clear look below. I had my field glasses and I took a long look through 'em.

"She's there, all right," I said to Yandle. "Both of 'em outside, at least."

"Doing what?"

"Tarbeaux's on the house roof, Mary Beth's handing wood and shingles up to him."

"So he's fixing the place up to stay."

"Or getting it ready to sell," I said. If selling wasn't what he had in mind, it would be sooner or later.

Yandle took off his hat, sleeved sweat off his forehead. He had the damnedest hair—long, scraggly, orange as a carrot except for streaks bleached almost white by the sun. He's not too bright, but he takes orders well enough and does what he's told without complaining.

"You think he got the money yet, Jada?"

"What money?"

"The money he stole and hid."

"Where'd you hear about that?"

"In town. Saloon talk. It's true, ain't it?"

"He wouldn't have gone to the pen if it wasn't."

"So you reckon he's got it now?"

I shrugged. "Depends on where he stashed it."

"Over five thousand dollars," Yandle said, and licked his lips. "Man, that's a lot of *dinero*."

"More'n you and I will ever see. But it's none of our concern unless he aims to spend it on Miss Mary Beth."

We went back to the horses and rode on down into the ranch yard. Miss Mary Beth was halfway up the ladder, Tarbeaux still on the roof. He didn't move as we drew rein and swung out of leather, but she climbed down and came stomping over to me. Her face was flushed red and shiny from the heat, her hair all sweated on her neck, and there was a streak of dirt on one cheek. She's got the Colonel's temper, and her eyes were hot and flashing with it now.

"What are you doing here? Following me?"

"Didn't need to. The Colonel don't want you here, Miss Mary Beth."

"I don't care what the Colonel wants. I'll tell you the same thing I told him: I go where I please and see who I please."

"He said if we found you here, we was to bring you home and don't take no for an answer."

"Well, you'd better take 'no' because I'm not leaving until I'm good and ready." The girl had spunk, you had to give her that. Spunk, but not a lick of sense when it come to men. Should've been married years ago, pretty as she was, give the Colonel the grandkids he hankered after, but no, she couldn't get Tarbeaux out of her head.

"You want us to hogtie you on your Appaloosa?"

"You wouldn't dare."

Tarbeaux was on the ladder now, coming down. He had a clawhammer in his hand and his face was set tight. "Leave the girl alone, Kinch."

Well, I never could abide him. Wild kid, then a thief, now an ex-con—hell, he wasn't fit to stand in her shadow. Hollow-eyed, prison pale, leaner than I remembered in dusty new Levi's and a linsey-woolsey shirt with the sleeves rolled up over his elbows. You could maybe figure what Miss Mary Beth seen in him five years ago, but now? He looked no better than a trail bum or one of those hardscrabble sodbusters that kept tearing up the land.

"Don't tell me what to do, jailbird," I said. "I take my orders from Colonel Greathouse."

"And lick his boots for him, too, same as always."

"You looking to start trouble with me?"

"That's the real reason you're here, isn't it? To make trouble?"

"We come to take Miss Greathouse home and tell you to stay clear of her from now on. You know what's good for you, you'll go get the money you stole if you ain't done it already—"

"Jim didn't steal that money!" Miss Mary Beth said, sharp.

"—and sell out and pull your freight."

"Maybe I'll sell, maybe I won't," Tarbeaux said. "Right now Keystone is mine and you're trespassing. Pull *your* freight."

"Not without Miss Greathouse."

"I told you, Jada," she snapped, "I'm not leaving until I'm ready."

"All right, then," I said. "Al, I reckon we'll have to do like I said. Go find her horse and we'll tie her on her side-saddle."

Tarbeaux said, like I expected and wanted him to, "You'll have to go through me."

I showed him my teeth the way a wolf does. "Well, that'll be a pure pleasure," and nodded to Yandle to go ahead.

Tarbeaux took a step sideways to block his way, the clawhammer coming up in his hand. Miss Mary Beth cried, "Jim, no!" I backed up a little, just enough so I'd have room to draw the Peacemaker if it came to that.

"You swing that hammer at either of us," I said, "it'll be the last thing you ever do. Self-defense, in front of witnesses."

"You'd like that, wouldn't you. I'm not that much of a fool." He let go of the hammer and it raised a puff of dust when it hit the ground. "You want a fight, unbuckle your gun belt."

"Why, sure. If that's how you want it."

"You're the one who wants it. You and the Colonel." He glanced sideways at Yandle. "Two against one?"

"Just you and me," I said. "I don't need no help with the likes of you."

I started to unbuckle. Tarbeaux was a dozen years younger than me, but I had more size and weight and the kind of savvy a man loses when he's been locked up in a cell for five years. No matter how much of a scrapper he was, I figured to cut him up good and proper.

But I didn't get the chance. Miss Mary Beth stomped her foot, hard, like a dauncy horse, and grabbed hold of Tarbeaux's arm. "No! There'll be no fighting."

"Stay out of this, Mary Beth," he said.

"I won't stay out of it. And I won't stand by and let it happen." She stepped away from him and said to me, "All right, Jada. I'll go with you."

Tarbeaux said, "You don't have to do that—"

"Yes I do. This time. I'll get Southwind." She put her back to us and stalked off toward the barn.

"There better not be a next time," I said to Tarbeaux. "You keep away from her long as you're here. If you don't—"

"What, Kinch? The two of you'll ambush me and beat hell out of me? Or back-shoot me some dark night?"

"I never shot a man in the back and never will. If I put a bullet in you, it'll be face-to-face and with legal cause."

SETH JENNISON

Some sort of hubbub over on Central Street woke me out of a half doze late Saturday morning. I hoisted myself out of my desk chair feeling a mite grumpy and went outside. Sounded like banjo music and singing, by golly. I walked up to the corner fast as the heat would allow, and got there just as the biggest, fanciest John Deere wagon I'd ever seen came clattering around the fenced-in box elder on the near side.

Folks were standing along the boardwalks or following after the wagon, staring same as I was. It was painted bright red with a shiny gold curlicue design, drawn by two large bays and so big and wide that the other conveyances in the street had to veer over to get out of its way. Curving red letters in the middle of the design, I saw as it passed me, spelled out **Doc Christmas, Painless Dentist**. Up on the seat were two of the oddest-looking gents a body was ever likely to set eyes on. The one holding the reins must've been four or five inches over six foot, shotgun thin, with a head big as a melon and chin whiskers all the way down the front of his black broadcloth coat. The other one, decked out in a mustard-yellow outfit, was half as tall, four times as wide, and bald as an egg, and he was strumming an outlandish large banjo and singing "Buffalo Gals" in a voice loud enough to rattle glass.

Well, we'd had our fair share of patent-medicine drummers in Box Elder, and once we'd even had a traveling medicine show that had a juggler and twelve trained dogs and sold an herb compound and catarrh cure that gave everybody that took it the trots. But we'd never had a painless dentist before.

Fact was, I'd never heard of Doc Christmas. Turned out nobody else had, either. He was brand-spanking new on the traveling circuit, and that made him all the more of a curiosity. He drove that gaudy wagon of his straight down Central, half the townsfolk and Saturday ranch and farm shoppers trailing after him like those German citizens was supposed to've trailed after the Pied Piper. Me, too, as much out of plain curiosity as because it was my job to keep the peace.

Somebody must've told Doc Christmas when he arrived about the willow flat along the river, where a town ordinance made it legal to camp for free except on Independence Day. He drove that wagon of his over onto the flat and parked it in a shady spot, its hind end facing at an off-angle toward town. Then him and the bald gent, whose name I came to find out later was Homer, opened up the back end and fiddled around until they had a kind of little stage with a painted curtain behind it. Then they got up on the stage together, and Homer played more tunes on his banjo while the two of 'em sang the words, all louder than they were melodious. Then Doc Christmas set out a display of instruments on a slant-board table, while Homer went around handing out penny candy to the kids and printed leaflets to the adults.

When I got hold of one of the leaflets, I saw it said in bold black letters that Doc Christmas was the Territory's newest and finest painless dentist, and the inventor of Doc Christmas's Wonder Painkiller, "the most precious boon to the oral health of mankind yet discovered." It said further that he'd dedicated his life to dispensing this fantastic new elixir, and to ridding his patients' mouths of loose and decayed teeth so the rest could remain healthy and harmonious. And at the last, in smaller print, there was a list of what his services cost.

A pint bottle of Doc Christmas's Wonder Painkiller, a three months' supply with judicious use—one dollar. A thorough dental examination—four bits for adults, children two bits unless they were under the age of six, in which case there was no charge. Cavity fillings per tooth—six bits for gold, four bits for something called "a special amalgam." Pulling of a loose or decayed tooth—one dollar for a simple extraction, three dollars for a difficult extraction that took more than five minutes. Bridgework and a partial or complete set of vulcanite false teeth—negotiable, depending on whether the patient could be fitted here and now from available stock or a special order was required, but guaranteed reasonable in any case. No other fees of any kind, and painless results likewise guaranteed.

"I wonder if he's half as good as he claims to be," the gent standing next to me said.

I'd seen him around a time or two lately, but I didn't know his name. "Who would you be?"

"Jones, Marshal. Artemas Jones."

Then I noticed his ink-stained hands and I said, "Oh, you're that printer fella just went to work for Will Satterlee. The one who—"

"The one who coldcocked me when I wasn't lookin' the other night."

That came from Elrod Patch, who shouldered up in front of Jones and stood glaring at him. One side of his face was all pooched up and the swelling gave his usually growly voice a kind of lisp. Then he said, "You had no call to blindside me the way you done," and poked the printer in the chest with one of his sausage fingers. "Busted off one of my back teeth."

Jones didn't flinch. Didn't answer or give ground, either, just stared back without blinking. Maybe it was because he was standing next to the law, but I didn't think so. I had the sense that he wouldn't back off from any man, even one as big and mean as Elrod Patch.

I said, "The way I heard it, Patch, he saved you from hurting the Rheinmiller boy enough to land you in jail."

He ignored me. "I'll be seeing you again, mister," he said to Jones, and moved off into the crowd.

"Disagreeable fellow, isn't he," Jones said.

"That's putting it mild." I'd arrested Patch seven or eight times on charges from drunk and disorderly to assault and battery to cheating customers like Hugo Rheinmiller to caving in the skull of Ben Coltrane's steeldust with a five-pound sledge. He'd been fined a few times, but that was all. Offended parties and witnesses had a peculiar way of dropping their complaints before it came time to face the circuit judge. "He's a mean cuss and he makes a bad enemy. I'd watch my back if I was you."

"I have been watching it, Marshal. You're not the first to warn me about Mr. Patch."

Up on the wagon, Doc Christmas had all his instruments laid out now. Homer quit playing his banjo, and the doc commenced his spiel in a voice surprisingly strong for such a beanpole of a man. He said pretty much the same things his leaflet said, only in words so eloquent any politician would've been proud to steal 'em for his own.

Then he said he was willing to demonstrate the fabulous power of his painkiller as a public service without cost to the first suffering citizen who volunteered to have a tooth drawn. Was there any poor soul here who had an aching molar or throbbing bicuspid? Doc Christmas invited him or her to step right up and be relieved.

I figured it might take more than that for him to get himself a customer, even one for free. Folks around here tend to be leery when it comes to strangers and newfangled painkillers, after the traveling medicine show's catarrh "cure." But I was wrong. His offer was taken up right away, and by two citizens, not just one.

The first to speak up was Orville Flowers, who owns the feed and grain store. He was standing close in front, and no sooner had Doc Christmas finished talking than Orville called out, "I volunteer! I've got a side molar that's been giving me fits for a month."

"Step up here with me, sir, right up here with Homer and me."

Orville got one foot on the wagon, but not the second, because just then Elrod Patch came barreling through the crowd, shouting in that funny half-lisping growl, "No you don't, Flowers! I got a worse swole-up mouth ache than you or any man ever had. My broke-up tooth is gonna be yanked first and yanked free and I ain't taking argument from you or anybody else."

Patch shoved Orville out of the way, even though it didn't look as though Flowers was fixing to argue. Then he climbed up on the stage, stood with his feet planted wide. "All right, sawbones," he said to Doc Christmas. "Pick up your tools and start yanking."

"I am not a doctor, sir. I am a painless dentist."

"All the same to me. Where do I sit?"

Doc Christmas fingered his whiskers. "The other gentleman volunteered first, Mister . . . ?"

"Elrod Patch, blacksmith, and I don't care if half of Box Elder volunteered first. I'm here, and I'm the one suffering the worst. Get to it. And it better be painless, too."

I could have stepped up on Orville Flowers's behalf, but the mood Patch was in, it would likely have meant trouble. And in a crowd like this, a third of 'em women and kids, trouble was the last thing I wanted. Doc Christmas didn't want any, either. He said to Patch, "Very well, sir," and made a signal to his assistant. Homer went behind the painted curtain, came out again with a chair like a cut-down barber's chair with a swivel mirror attached to it, and a long horizontal rod at the top—to hold a lantern for nighttime work, I supposed. He put the chair down next to the table that held the dentist's instruments.

Patch squeezed his bulk into the chair. Doc Christmas opened up Patch's mouth with one long-fingered hand, poked and prodded some inside, then picked up a funny-looking tool and poked and prodded with that. He did it real gentle. Patch squirmed some, but didn't make a sound the whole time.

Homer came over with a bottle of the wonder pain-killer, and Doc Christmas held it up to show the crowd while he did some more orating on its virtues. Then he un-stoppered it and swabbed some thick brown liquid inside Patch's mouth. Once he was done with that, Homer handed him a pair of forceps, which the doc brandished for the crowd. That painkiller of his sure appeared to be doing what it was advertised to do, for Patch was sitting quiet in the chair with a less hostile look on his ugly face.

Things didn't stay quiet for long, though. All of a sudden Homer took up his banjo and commenced to play and sing "Camptown Races" real loud. And with more strength than you'd figure a man with his frame would have, Doc Christmas grabbed Patch around the head with his hand tight over the windpipe, shoved the forceps into his wide-open maw, got a grip on the busted tooth, and started yanking.

It looked to me like Patch was yelling something fierce, the way his legs were kicking and his arms flapping. But Homer's banjo playing and singing were too loud to hear anything else. Doc Christmas yanked, and Patch struggled for what must've been about a minute and a half. Then the doc let go of his windpipe and with a flourish he held up the forceps, at the end of which was the bloody remains of a snaggletooth.

Patch tried to get up out of the chair. Doc Christmas shoved him back down, took a big wad of cotton off the table, swabbed some more painkiller on it, and poked it into Patch's mouth. When he did that, Homer quit picking and caterwauling, and as soon as it was quiet, the doc said to the crowd, "A simple, painless extraction, ladies and gentlemen, accomplished in less time than it takes to peel and core an apple. It was painless, was it not, Mr. Patch?"

The blacksmith was on his feet now. He seemed wobbly and dazed. He tried to say something, but with all that cotton in his mouth the words came out garbled and thick so you couldn't understand them. Homer and Doc Christmas handed him down off the wagon. Folks parted fast as Patch weaved his way through, giving him plenty of room.

He passed close to me on his way out to the track, and he looked some stunned.

The printer, Jones, said through a grin, "Doc Christmas's Wonder Painkiller sure must be a marvel of medical science."

Once Patch was out of the way, folks began applauding and pushing closer to the wagon. In the next half hour, Doc Christmas pulled Orville Flowers's bad tooth—Orville didn't kick up any more fuss than Patch had—and gave a couple of four-bit dental examinations, and Homer sold five bottles of the painkiller. I bought a pint myself. I figured it was the least I could do in appreciation for the show they'd put on and that stunned look on Patch's face when he passed me by.

JIM TARBEAUX

The face-off with Kinch had made up my mind for me. I was not about to give in to pressure from Colonel Greathouse or anybody else, put my tail between my legs and run like a whipped dog. I was not going to sell Keystone. I was all through being pushed around and treated like dirt. I intended to stick on the land I'd been born and raised on, and to protect it and myself come hell or high water. Make the ranch pay again somehow, no matter how long it took, and when I felt I could afford to have a wife and family, then I would marry Mary Beth, and her father and the rest of the haters be damned.

I wanted to talk over my decision with her, but not at Keystone. She wasn't to come there any more, it would only provoke trouble. We'd have to get together on the sly for a while. So I'd written her a note asking her to meet me tomorrow any time she could get away after noon, at the place where we used to rendezvous before Cable framed me. I had the paper folded in my shirt pocket when I rode into Box Elder.

The town was surprisingly empty for a Saturday. Something going on on the willow flat by the river, judging from the banjo playing and loud singing coming from that direction. Nothing for me to bother with, whatever it was.

I stopped first at the livery to return the roan horse and pay Sam Benson the additional money I owed him for the rental. When I told him I was definitely planning to stay on, he didn't seem surprised or put out about it; he agreed to let me buy the saddle and a chestnut gelding for five dollars down and two dollars a month. The chestnut would serve as both saddle and wagon horse. Pa's old buckboard was in the barn at Keystone, still in serviceable condition, or would be once I tightened the wheel nuts and greased the axles.

The gunsmith's shop came next. The owner now was a man I didn't know, and that was just as well. I bargained with him for a secondhand Springfield rifle that he must have had for a while, given the price he settled on, and a box of shells. A sidearm would have to wait until I could afford one.

The only person in Prairie Mercantile when I entered was Etta Lohrman, Mary Beth's best friend, who clerked there. Etta was glad to see me and glad to deliver my note to Mary Beth tonight, just as she'd been glad to mail Mary Beth's letters to me in Deer Lodge and pass on mine sent care of her in return. She was a nice, homely girl, as yet unmarried, and I guess acting as a secret go-between had put some savor into her life.

With what little money I had left I bought a few essentials—flour, beans, coffee, a small slab of bacon—and while Etta sacked them she told me that the hubbub down on the flat had sprung from the arrival of a painless dentist and patent-medicine drummer in a fancy yellow and red wagon. Most folks find that type of visitor a welcome diversion, but I wouldn't have cared if I'd had an impacted wisdom tooth. I tied the grocery sacks to the saddle horn, then rode to Cable's shop.

The time had come for a showdown. I'd waited long enough. Before I could hope to settle in the basin without being shunned I *had* to clear my name. Cable was the one who'd sullied it; he was the only one who could restore it.

He was there, working in a halfhearted, distracted way at his cutting bench. He jerked when he saw me come in, then went stiff, his eyes widening and glistening with what I took to be fear. An old double-barreled shotgun leaned against the wall near him; he made a grab for it, swung it up. But he didn't quite aim it at me, the barrels pointed at an off angle to my left. I held my hands out away from my body, palms toward him.

He made a throat-clearing sound, but he didn't say anything for several seconds. In the glow from an Argand lamp hung above the table, he looked small and shrunken. His sweat-pocked skin was sallow, pinched, and his hands weren't steady. He'd aged fifteen years in the past five.

Finally he said, "I heard you were back, Jim," in a low voice that wobbled a little.

"Expecting me, I see."

"I knew you'd come. Took your time about it."

"I had other things to do. You fixing to shoot me with that scattergun?"

"If you fill your hand, I will. Both barrels."

"I'm not armed."

"Expect me to believe that?"

I shrugged and glanced slowly around the shadowed room. "Pretty fair leatherwork. Seems you were cut out to be a saddle maker, like you always wanted."

"Man's got to do something."

"That's a fact. Only thing is, he ought to do it with honest money."

"All right," Cable said.

"All right what? You finally ready to admit you stole the Kendalls' money?"

He didn't say anything. But his eyes were furtive, haunted.

"You know, it's a funny thing," I said. "A man can be in prison even when there's no bars on his windows."

"I don't know what you're talking about."

"Sure you do. It's been a hard five years for you, too. Harder, in some ways, than the ones I lived through."

Again no reply.

"You were on a downhill slide even before you bought this shop and learned the trade. Starting with Clara Davis. You always talked about marrying her, having three or four kids . . . your other big ambition. But she turned you down when you asked for her hand. Married a storekeeper in Billings instead."

The words made Cable's hands twitch on the shotgun. "How do you know that?"

Mary Beth had written me about it. Other things about Cable, too. "I know plenty about you, Rufus, never mind how. You proposed to another woman; she wouldn't have you, either. Then you lost a fair amount in a bad mining-stock investment. Then one of your horses kicked over a lantern and burned down your barn. Then you caught consumption and were laid up in bed for more than a month—"

"That's enough," Cable said, but there was no heat in his voice. Only a kind of desperate weariness.

"The hell it is. Your health's been poor ever since, worsening steadily, and there's nothing much the doctors can do about it. How much more time do you reckon you have? Two years, three?"

"Addled, whoever told you that. I'm healthy enough. I've got a long life ahead of me."

"No, I'm the one with the long life ahead. And I intend it to be a good life, right here in Box Elder."

"That won't happen. You're not welcome here, not after what people believe you did."

"I'll make myself welcome. Rebuild Keystone, rebuild my reputation, no matter how long it takes. How do you like the idea of having me for a neighbor again?"

"I don't, damn you. You better settle with me before you think about doing anything else."

"That's right. First I have to settle with you."

"Kill me, like you swore in court you'd do."

"I never swore that."

"Same as."

"You think I still hate you that much?"

"Don't you?"

"No. Not any more."

"I don't believe that. You're lying."

"You're the liar, Rufus, not me."

"You want me dead. Admit it . . . you want me dead."

"You'll be dead soon enough to suit me."

"You can't stand to wait. You want me dead *now*."

"Wrong. All I ever wanted was for you to pay for what you did to me and admit the truth. Well, you're paying and paying dear—that's one part of the settlement."

"You can't make me confess."

"Yes I can. A public admission of guilt."

"No. I couldn't face prison, couldn't stand being locked up."

"I stood it for five years," I said.

"You couldn't beat a confession out of me five years ago, you couldn't do it now. I'll never confess. You hear me? Never!" Cable ran his tongue over dry, cracked lips. "Now draw your weapon and get it over with."

"I told you, I'm not armed."

He jerked the scattergun up, jabbing with it—a gesture meant to be provoking. But his hands shook so much he couldn't hold it straight. "Go on, you son of a bitch, kill me, get it over with!"

Understanding broke in on me then. There was no fight

in Cable, no resistance, the attempt at provocation as meaningless as it was desperate. There was only fear, guilt, a hopeless resignation. He had lost more than money, more than his health; he had lost the will to live.

"You *want* me to kill you," I said. "That's it, isn't it? You want me to put you out of your misery."

It was as if I'd slapped him across the face. His head jerked, his eyes bulged; he took a step toward me, jabbing again with the shotgun. I didn't move. There was no need to defend myself.

"You can't stand the thought of slowly wasting away, but you don't have the guts to finish yourself off. You figured I'd do it for you, goad me into it if necessary."

"No!"

"That scattergun isn't loaded. It's as empty as you are."

Cable tried to stare me down. The effort lasted no more than a few seconds. His gaze slid down to the useless shotgun; then, as if the weight of it was too much for his shaking hands, he let it fall to the floor, kicked it clattering under the workbench.

"Why?" he said in a thin, hollow whisper. "Why couldn't you do what you vowed you'd do? Why couldn't you finish it?"

"That part is finished," I said. "All that's left is for you to tell the truth, and you will sooner or later. You won't have a minute's peace until you do, I'll see to that."

I put my back to him and walked out.

DOC CHRISTMAS

I was relieved to find the town marshal's office open for business on a Sunday morning. Of course church services are held early in such provincial settlements as Box Elder, and lawbreakers and disturbers of the peace have little respect for the Sabbath. The marshal's name, according to a sign on the door, was Seth Jennison. I straightened my coat, adjusted my hat, smoothed the brush on my chin, and entered.

The man seated at a cluttered desk—Marshal Jennison, a fact attested to by the star on his vest—was a large, sturdy individual of some forty summers, his ovoid head devoid of hair except for a thin ruff above the ears and two patches like tiny grass hummocks at the crest. I recalled seeing him among the other citizens gathered on the river flat upon Homer's and my arrival in Box Elder. There was an air of calm authority about him, an unflappability, that I found reassuring. Some guardians of the law are less than accommodating to a man in my noble profession, judging me solely on the somewhat unorthodox but effective methods of attracting patients that Homer and I choose to employ in our travels.

"Well, now, Doc Christmas," he said. If he was surprised to find me in his domain, he showed no indication of it. "What can I do for you?"

"I wish to lodge a complaint."

"That so? What kind of complaint?"

"One of the citizens of your community threatened my life some twenty minutes ago. My assistant Homer's life as well. In no uncertain terms, I may add."

"Who did the threatening?" he asked, but I had the sense from the furrowing of his brow and the tightening of his jaw that he knew the answer before I gave it.

"The blacksmith, Elrod Patch."

"Uh-huh."

"The man is a philistine," I said.

"Won't get no argument from me on that. Philistine, troublemaker, and holy terror. What'd he threaten you and Homer for? Body'd think he'd be grateful after you yanked his bad tooth free of charge."

"He claims it was not the painless extraction I guaranteed."

"Oh, he does."

"It is his contention that he suffered grievously the entire night, and that he is still in severe pain this morning. I explained to him that some discomfort is natural after a difficult extraction, and that, if he had paid heed to my lecture, he would have understood the necessity of purchasing an entire bottle of my Wonder Painkiller. Had he done so, he would have slept the sleep of an innocent babe and be fit as a fiddle today."

"What'd he say to that?"

"He insisted that I should have supplied a bottle gratis. I informed him again that only the public extraction was gratis, but he refused to listen."

"Just one of his many faults."

"He demanded a free bottle. Naturally I did not knuckle under to what amounted to a blatant attempt at extortion."

"Naturally. That when he threatened your life?"

"In foul and abusive language."

"Uh-huh. Any witnesses?"

"Other than Homer, no. We three were alone at the wagon."

"Well then, sir, I'm afraid there's not much I can do unless he actually laid a hand on you or Homer. Did he?"

"No," I admitted, "not then. Is he as violent as he appears to be?"

"He can be, though mostly he's a big wind. Far as I know he's never killed anybody human, just a horse once, so it's unlikely he'll follow up on his threat."

"But he would go so far as to subject Homer and myself to physical abuse, would he not? And/or to damage my wagon and equipment?"

"He might, if he was riled enough. He threaten to do that, too, bust up your wagon?"

"He did."

Marshal Jennison sighed. "I'll have a talk with him, Doc, try to settle him down. But he don't like me and I don't like him, so I doubt it'll do much good. How long you fixing to camp in Box Elder?"

"Business was brisk last evening," I said, which was not exactly the truth. "We anticipate it will be likewise today and perhaps tomorrow as well, once word spreads of my dental skill and the stupendous properties of my Wonder Painkiller."

"I don't suppose you'd consider cutting your visit short and moving on somewhere else?"

I drew myself up. "I would not, sir. Doc Christmas flees before the wrath of no man."

"I was afraid of that. Uh, how long you reckon Patch's mouth will hurt without he treats it with more of your painkiller?"

"The exact length of time varies from patient to patient. A day, two days, perhaps as long as a week."

The marshal sighed again, a bit gustily this time, I thought. "I was afraid of that, too," he said.

MARY BETH GREATHOUSE

Getting away to meet Jim was considerably easier on Sunday than it would've been any other day. When Mother was alive she made the Colonel attend church services sometimes, but he was not religious and had not gone once since she died. But he had no objection to me going. I'd arranged with Etta when she delivered Jim's note to come by and pick me up early Sunday morning, and Father didn't suspect a thing when I told him. I said the reason I was taking my picnic basket along was that Etta and I intended to have our lunch down by the river afterward; he didn't question that, either, hadn't a clue that my riding clothes were bundled up inside.

Etta and I went to church, endured one of Reverend Harper's antisin sermons, and afterward rode to her house where she lived with her brother Tom. She'd have let me borrow her buggy, but the only way to get to where I was going was on horseback. She had a way of wrapping Tom around her little finger, and she talked him into lending me his piebald for the afternoon. The horse wasn't nearly as fleet or sure-footed as Southwind, but it felt good to sit astride a regular saddle instead of the sidesaddle the Colonel insisted I use. He would have had a conniption fit if he knew I no longer needed it for the reason he thought I did, and hadn't since a month or so before Jim was railroaded into prison.

Our old rendezvous spot was up near the Knob, where a network of narrow, shallow, brush-filled coulees crisscrossed the high ground—a little-used part of open-range cattle graze before the horrible winter two years ago. There were so many cattle back then that some wandered up that way and got themselves lost or trapped; hundreds had died in those coulees seeking shelter and forage in vain during the string of blizzards. One of these days nesters might stake their claims there, too, though it would be a hardscrabble life for those that did; there was little water for irrigation that far up and away from the river.

Valley Road took me most of the way, old cattle trails the rest. Cowhands used to ride up there every now and then to hunt strays, but mostly the section was deserted. No one other than Jim and me had cause to go there any more.

I had explored the high ground along the base of the Knob often enough to know it well, and had found a favorite spot—a kind of bowl-shaped grotto where one of the smaller coulees pinched into a dead end. The ground in the grotto was mostly flat, sandy smooth, with a little spring along one side where chokecherries grew among the rocks.

The only way into it was through a declivity so narrow neither cows nor horses could squeeze through; even a big
man like Jim had to turn sideways. Coyotes, swift foxes,
marmots, and other small animals came there to drink in
spring and early summer—you could tell from their paw
prints—but you hardly ever saw one in the daytime. You
couldn't ask for a more private place.

Jim's horse—a different one than he'd had before, a
chestnut gelding—was picketed under a rocky overhang
outside the entrance. I left Tom's mare beside him, first untying the blanket from behind the saddle, then stepped
through the declivity and straight into Jim's arms. He
started to say something, but I stopped it with a kiss, and
not a chaste one, either. I had done nothing since Etta
brought his message but think about being with him
again here. We'd been alone together at Keystone, but he'd
been preoccupied and busy and there hadn't been much
passion in our embraces, at least not on his part. Now I
could feel it stirring in him the way it was in me.

But then he stood me off at arm's length and said, "Easy,
now, girl. We're here to talk."

"Not about what happened the other day?"

"Partly. I don't want you coming to Keystone any more,
for both our sakes."

"All right. Then we'll meet here from now on."

"But not often enough to make anyone suspicious. The
most important thing right now is to avoid trouble."

"You've decided to stay, then."

"It's the only way, Mary Beth. Going away with you would be a mistake we'd both regret. I won't be driven off my land by your father or anyone else, and I won't rest until my name is cleared."

He told me about his confrontation with Rufus Cable. "I don't relish the thought of hounding a sick man, but I will until he breaks and confesses."

"You really think he will?"

"I do. It's a matter of time and pressure. Just knowing I'm around, watching and waiting, will prey on his mind."

"But what if he works up enough nerve to come after you with a *loaded* shotgun?"

"He won't. It took all the guts he has to face me with it unloaded, hoping I'd kill him."

"And meanwhile?" I said. "It will take money to rebuild Keystone, a lot of money. Where will you get it?"

"I'm going to look for a job, starting tomorrow."

"Oh, Jim . . ."

"I know anything I can get right now won't be much, but it'll be a start."

"If you'd only let me help . . ."

"No. We've been all through that. I won't take handouts from you or friends of yours. I have to do it on my own."

"But it could take a long time . . . months, years. What about us, meanwhile?"

"We'll keep seeing each other whenever we can."

"Up here once a week or so. That's not enough for me. Or for you."

"It has to be. We can't get married right away, you know that."

"Why can't we? The Colonel wouldn't have to know about it. No one would."

"Sneak off to Billings, do it on the sly? No. Somebody would be sure to find out about it, and that'd just make things harder on both of us. I want to marry you, more than anything, but when I do the time and the situation have to be right."

Lord, he could be stubborn! But there was no use arguing with him when his mind was made up. I stepped away from him, shook the blanket open, and spread it out in chokecherry shade next to the spring—dry now, its bottom webbed with cracks.

As intent as Jim was, he hadn't noticed the blanket before. He said, "Why you'd bring that?"

"To sit on, why do you think. Are you hungry?"

"Hungry? I don't know . . . I didn't bring any food."

"I did."

I went out to Tom's horse, fetched the little bundle wrapped in waxed paper from the saddlebag—the picnic basket was too bulky to bring—and took it back into the grotto. I sat on the blanket, and after a few seconds Jim sat beside me. Not close enough to suit me; I scooted over until my hip touched his. "Cold fried chicken and hardboiled eggs, thanks to Etta," I said, but I didn't unwrap the bundle yet. "We'll eat in a little while."

"Why not now?"

I slid over next to him and showed him why not now. I slid my arms around him and pressed my body against his and kissed him, a long, hard, wet kiss that I could tell left him as shaken as it did me. It had been so long!

But he said, thick-tongued, "No, we'd better not."

"Why?"

"You know why. What if . . . well . . ."

"I didn't get caught five years ago."

"Lucky thing you didn't. We have to be sensible. We—"

I caught his hand and put it on my breast. He tried to draw it away, but I held it tight, looking into his eyes, my breath coming quick and unsteady.

"Mary Beth, no . . ."

"Jim, yes."

And I had my way.

SETH JENNISON

It was hellfire hot in the blacksmith shop, at least fifteen degrees hotter than the day outside. Patch stood banging away on a red-hot horseshoe with his five-pound sledge, drenched in sooty sweat, when I walked in. Wearing his mule-hide shoeing apron and getting ready to shoe a skewbald stallion waiting in the stall. He hammered with a vengeance, as if it was Doc Christmas's head forked there on his anvil. The whole left side of his ugly face was swelled up something wicked, about twice the size it'd been yesterday.

He glared when he saw me. "What in hell you want, Jennison?" The words didn't come out in a lisp as they had in the willow flat, but in a kind of snarly mumble that you had to pay close attention to understand.

"A few peaceable words, is all."

"Got nothing to say to you. My mouth hurts too much to talk." Then, Patch being Patch, he went ahead and jawed to me anyway. "Look at what that gawdamn tooth puller done to me. Hurts twice as bad without the tooth than it done with it in."

"Well, you did volunteer to have it yanked."

"I didn't volunteer for no swole-up face like I got now. Painless dentist, hell!"

"It's my understanding you threatened Doc Christmas and his assistant with bodily harm."

"Run to you, did he?" Patch said. "Well, it'd serve both of 'em right if I blowed their heads off with my twelve-gauge."

"You'd hang, Patch, and you know it."

He tried to scowl, but it pained his face and made him wince. He gave the horseshoe another lick with his sledge, then picked it up with a pair of tongs and dropped it into a bucket of water. Watching it steam and sizzle, he said, "There's other ways to skin a cat."

"Meaning?"

"Just what I said. Other ways to skin a cat."

"Patch, you listen to me. You do so much as harm a hair on Doc Christmas's or Homer's head, or damage that wagon of theirs, I'll slap you in jail and see you stay locked up as long as the law allows."

"I ain't afraid of you, Jennison."

"Ought to be, if you know what's good for you." I said it quiet, but as hard underneath as that iron horseshoe in the bucket.

"I know what's good for me right now—some of that bastard's painkiller. It's the genuine article, even if he ain't. And I aim to get me a bottle."

"Now, that's the first sensible thing I heard you say.

Whyn't you and me mosey on down to their wagon so's you can buy one."

"Buy? I ain't gonna *buy* something I should've got for nothing."

"Oh, Lordy, Patch. Doc Christmas never promised you a free bottle of his painkiller. All he promised was to draw your busted tooth at no charge, which he did."

"One's free, so's the other," Patch said. "Ain't nobody cheats Elrod Patch and gets away with it. Nobody!"

Well, that was some ironical coming from the biggest cheater in Box Elder, but I didn't say so. Just wasn't any use trying to talk sense to the man. I'd have got more satisfaction wasting my breath on a cottonwood stump. But I gave it one last try before I took myself out of his contrary company.

"You're warned, mister," I said. "Stay away from Doc Christmas and Homer and their wagon while they're in my jurisdiction. And that goes for Artemas Jones, too."

"Who?"

"The printer fella you half threatened in my hearing yesterday."

He curled the half of his lip that wasn't swollen. All it did was pull his grimy mustache out of shape and give him a comical lopsided look. "Another bastard," he said. "Cold-cocked me when I wasn't looking."

"With good cause, according to witnesses. Keep your distance from him, too. You'll damn well regret it if you don't."

All I got for an answer was a mutter and a snort. And then a look at his fat backside as he turned toward the forge.

It was too hot and I was too sweat-simmered myself to go anywhere but the Occidental House for a cold beer. As cold as you can get in Box Elder in the summer, Tate Reynolds not being stingy when it comes to buying ice to pack his kegs. Ned Foley wasn't behind the plank today, Sunday being his day off, which was too bad because he'd have been cheerful company while I had my beer; Ned's one of my oldest friends, and almost as good a cribbage player as I am. The bartender today was Ed Smeed, who always looked as if he had a bellyache and was about as talkative as a mule. There wasn't anybody among the other few customers I felt like conversing with, so I stood off by myself to sip my beer. Which didn't quite quench my thirst, so I decided there wouldn't be any harm in having another.

I'd almost finished that one when I had my inspiration. Or what seemed like one at the time.

I went home to Madge Tolliver's boardinghouse and upstairs to my room for the bottle of Doc Christmas's Wonder Painkiller I'd bought. Outside again, I spied the Ames boy, Tommy, rolling his hoop. I gave Tommy a nickel to take the bottle to the blacksmith's shop. I said he should tell Patch it was from Doc Christmas and that it was a peace offering, free of charge. Most of the time I don't hold with lying or having youngsters fib for me, but in this case I figured I was on the side of the angels and it was a pardonable sin in order to forestall trouble. Sometimes the only way to deal with the devil is by using his own methods.

Tommy reported back to me in the marshal's office. Took him three times as long as it should have; that was because Patch had been away from the shop and he had to wait for him to come back. "He took the bottle all right, Marshal. But then he laughed real nasty and said he suspicioned it was from you, not Doc Christmas."

Blast him for a sly fox, I thought, annoyed.

"He said now he had *two* bottles of painkiller, and his mouth didn't hurt no more, but it didn't make a lick of difference in how he felt toward that, um, blankety-blank tooth puller."

"Two bottles?"

"Yes, sir. He got the other from Mr. Flowers."

"Did he, now. By coercion, I'll warrant."

"What's coercion?"

"Never mind about that." Orville was a good man but he didn't have much sand; afraid of his own shadow. If Patch had coerced him, he'd never call him to task for it. "What else did Patch have to say?"

"Nothing. He just told me to go roll my hoop, so I did."

I left the office and stumped down to the willow flat to see Doc Christmas. There were only a few people around his wagon, it being late afternoon by this time. He had a farmer in the chair, one of the Jorgensen clan, and was yanking a tooth while Homer played his banjo and sang

"Camptown Races" at the top of his voice. I waited until they were done and three more bottles of the wonder pain-killer had been sold. Then I signaled the doc to come down, drew him off to one side, and told him what Patch had said to me and to Tommy Ames.

It didn't seem to bother him much. He fluffed up his chin whiskers and said, "As I told you yesterday, Marshal, Homer and I refuse to be intimidated by a philistine such as Elrod Patch."

"A dangerous philistine. My advice is for you to pull up stakes and move on tonight. Next time you come to Box Elder, if you ever do, Patch'll likely have forgotten his grudge."

"That would be the cowards' way, and Homer and I are men, not spineless whelps. The law and the Almighty can send us fleeing, but no man can without just cause."

Well, he had a point, and I couldn't argue with it. Couldn't order him to leave, either. He was on public land and he hadn't broken any laws, including the Almighty's so far as I knew. I wished him well and trudged back into town.

But I felt uneasy in my mind and a little tight in my bones. There was going to be trouble, sure as God made little green apples, and there wasn't any legal or even shifty-smart way I could see to stop it.

RUFUS CABLE

I spent half of Saturday and all day Sunday in bed, sick as a dog. Fever sweats, coughing spells, puking up what little I tried to drink and eat. All the symptoms of ague, but it wasn't ague. Or the consumption flaring up again, either.

It was Tarbeaux. A reaction to the way he'd shamed me in the shop, refused to carry out his vengeance threat when he realized the shotgun was empty—and the different vow he'd made. He had seen to it that I would continue to face a slow, frightening death, and he would make sure I didn't have a moment's peace until then.

Would he spread the word that I had tried to make him shoot me? Probably. Not many would believe him, but some would. I'd never been well thought of in Box Elder, before or after the trial. No real friends, no family since Ma died, no decent woman after Clara spurned me in favor of that Billings storekeeper. Just a hotel clerk turned saddle maker, never mind a good one once, who nobody paid much mind to, who kept to himself and lived alone in the house he'd hoped to fill with a wife and kids, who watched all his dreams die like dust devils in the wind. Nobody who gave a damn whether Rufus Cable lived or died. Including Rufus Cable himself.

But it mattered how and when and where I died. I didn't have to stay on here with Tarbeaux as a constant nemesis. I could sell the saddle shop for whatever I could get, move to Billings . . . no, not Billings, not with Clara there. Clear out of Montana entirely, head down to New Mexico or Arizona. The doctors had told me I might have a chance to live a while longer in that kind of hot, dry climate. Not recover my health, just live another year or two. Maybe. No guarantees.

I'd tried and failed to talk myself into selling and moving before Tarbeaux came back. Now it was too late. I was in no condition for that kind of long travel, or the effort it would take to establish myself and my business in a strange place. And even if I could manage it, would what was left of my life be any different there than it was here? Would I fit in any better, make friends, meet a woman willing to keep company with a dying consumptive? Would my slow death be any easier? No. Hell, no.

Stuck in Box Elder for however much time I had left. That would be barely tolerable, but not with Tarbeaux hounding me every chance he had. But I wouldn't confess, not even if he tried again to beat it out of me. If he laid a hand on me, I would press a charge of attempted murder and have him sent back to Deer Lodge. He knew that, he was no fool. No, he'd do his hounding with words and visits. And my God, the unbearable strain that would put on me!

The only slim hopes I had were that something would happen to change his mind, drive him out of the basin for good, or that he would have a fatal accident or be killed some other way. *Him* dying was the best solution of all.

I wished again that I had the guts to kill him. I'd thought about it often enough, of ambushing him as soon as he showed up, but all the thinking did was make my belly churn and my hands sweat. I couldn't do it. Couldn't pull a trigger on him even in self-defense. And even if I could, Jennison or the county law would surely find out and I'd be arrested and sentenced to hang. Hanging wasn't a fast, easy way to die . . . not when you were locked up for days or weeks beforehand, waiting and watching the gallows being built.

A bullet was a fast way to die, the best way. It had taken all the nerve I have to face him with the unloaded shotgun. And when the time seemed to finally come yesterday, I had been so scared I nearly pissed my pants. I couldn't go through that again, either. And Tarbeaux knew I couldn't.

I wished to Christ he was still in Deer Lodge, that the judge had sentenced him to ten or twenty years instead of just five. If he were in prison, I wouldn't be sick in bed like this, I wouldn't have to live with this awful sickening fear . . .

That was when the notion came to me.

It was a crazy notion, but I couldn't get it out of my head. I *could* do that, I thought. And why not, after the way I've been treated and will be treated if I don't? The sacrifice was a small enough price to pay, and there was a way to minimize the loss. What I had to do was plan it out carefully before I went ahead. Do it right and nobody would suspect me, the victim once again, the eyewitness.

Studying on it, planning it, I didn't feel sick any more. Pull this off, and I would be free of Tarbeaux once and for all. And I could live out the time I had left with a measure of peace.

HOMER ST. JOHN

Doc Christmas and me was setting around the campfire behind our John Deere wagon, waiting for the pork belly and 'taters to finish roasting, Doc smoking his pipe and sipping coffee, me strumming a quiet tune on my banjo, when this fella come moseying along the riverbank over by where we'd picketed the horses. Couldn't tell who he was at first. Full dark now, the moon not up yet, and the firelight wasn't bright enough to cut through the shadows under the low-hanging willow branches.

Doc tensed up. And I quit strumming. Both of us remembering the threats that big angry blacksmith, Patch, had made. I'm a yard wide myself, and strong enough when needs be, like having to lift up the wagon when one of the wheels loosens up or gets stuck in mud, but I ain't much of a fighter. No, sir, not me. Mama used to call me her soft, sweet boy when I was a button in Spokane. Well, she had the soft part right, anyway. That blacksmith was half fat and half brawn. Me, I'm all blubber.

But when the fella come out of the shadows into the firelight and Doc and me both seen it wasn't Patch, we took our ease again. I didn't know who he was, but I'd seen him in the crowd when we first set up here on Saturday afternoon. One thing about me besides being a fair to middlin' banjo player, I got a good memory for faces. And a good memory for who buys Doc Christmas's Wonder Painkiller and who doesn't. This fella was one who hadn't.

"Evening," he says.

Doc says, "Evening. We're closed for business, sir, and preparing a late evening meal. Unless, of course, you are in dire need of my services, for which there is an extra after-hours charge, or you wish to purchase a bottle of my wonder painkiller."

"Neither one."

I couldn't resist saying, "You didn't buy a bottle last time you was here, either."

"No need. I'm not in pain, mouth or otherwise."

"Toothaches come on unexpected sometimes. Good idea to keep a bottle handy."

"No doubt, but I'll only be in Box Elder a short while. And I like to travel light." His nose twitched like a hound keening the air. "Whatever you're cooking there sure does smell good."

"Roasted 'taters and pork belly."

Doc says, quick, "I believe in hospitality, sir, but I regret to say that I can't invite you to join us. There is only enough victuals for Homer and me."

"Oh, I wasn't fishing for an invitation. I've already eaten. Out for a stroll to aid my digestion and I heard Homer's banjo. 'The Girl I Left Behind Me' is one of my favorite tunes."

"Indeed."

"You play it well, Homer," he says to me. "Much more harmoniously than 'Camptown Race' or 'Buffalo Gals,' if you don't mind my saying so."

I wasn't offended. Fact is fact and no denying it. "The quieter the tune," I says, "the better I strum."

"Mind playing it again?"

"Don't see why not. 'Taters ain't quite ready yet."

I commenced to strum, and danged if he didn't whip a harmonica out of his sack-coat pocket and join in. He wasn't exactly a sure hand—or sure mouth—with the instrument, but then again he didn't play too bad, either. Matter of fact, the two of us playing and then singing together give "The Girl I Left Behind Me" a kind of sad sound a mite different than me and my banjo done alone.

Doc Christmas clapped his hands when we was finished. "Well done," he says, which along with the clapping is some compliment from him. "You know our names, sir. Yours, may I ask?"

"Artemas Jones. Printer by trade, rolling stone by nature."

Well, that was us, too, Doc and me. Rolling stones. For three years now as long as the weather permitted, ever since he'd invented his wonder painkiller and decided to sublet his practice in Spokane and take his business and his invention on the road. He was a queer old bird, Doc was. All that mattered to him these days was traveling to parts he'd never been before, fixing folks' teeth in small towns like Box Elder that didn't have a dentist, and salting away as much from doing that and from his painkiller as he could. Once he'd satisfied the wanderlust that'd come on him late in life, he figured on going back to Spokane permanent, instead of just to winter there like we was doing now, and open up a dental school.

Except for being some tightfisted, he didn't give me no cause for complaint. I liked working for him; he treated me more like a friend than his assistant. He'd needed somebody to help him manufacture the elixir, which you could do on the road with ingredients that wasn't too hard to get hold of, and to assist with his pitch and dental work. That was how I come to join up with him. So far we'd traveled eastern Washington, the Idaho panhandle, and most of Montana, with the Dakotas and Wyoming on the horizon. It was a good life, mostly. Except when we run into somebody like that ornery yahoo Patch, but that didn't happen too often. Most customer grievances I took care of with hardly any problem. I may not be a fighter, but I can put on a real fierce look and growl like a bear when I set my mind to it, and my three hundred pounds takes care of the rest.

"A kindred spirit," Doc says to this fella Jones. "How long have you been obeying the call of the open road?"

"More than a dozen years now. And you?"

"Not long enough. I can't offer you provender, as I said, but there is plenty of coffee if you'd care for a cup."

"I would at that, thanks."

He sat down and I poured him one. He took a sip and says right off, "Arbuckles'."

"You know your coffee, sir."

"I know the best when I have a chance to drink it."

So we set there and drank coffee and traded road stories until the 'taters and pork belly was ready. Jones had traveled all over the country, seemed like, places that was only rumors to me—and he was brimful of stories, some of 'em funny. One in particular about doings in a bawdy house in Kansas City even made Doc laugh, which he don't do too often.

I'd've liked to hear more of Jones's yarns, but I was more interested right then in filling the hole in my stomach. Soon as I started to take the vittles off the fire, my mouth watering something fierce, he says, "Well, I'll leave you gents to your supper." Then he thanked us for the coffee and went on his way along the riverbank, where he commenced to play a different tune on his harmonica. "The Girl with the Blue Velvet Band," I thought it was.

"Nice fella," I says, setting the 'taters and pork belly out to cool enough so we wouldn't burn our mouths when we dug in.

"Indeed," Doc says. "A kindred spirit as I stated earlier. There is, however, one thing wrong with him."

"He didn't buy a bottle of your wonder painkiller."

"Precisely. No man should be as healthy in mouth and body as Mr. Artemas Jones."

ELROD PATCH

I finished off the second bottle of painkiller some past nightfall. Trouble with the stuff was, it killed the ache in my mouth well enough for a spell, but it didn't last for long. By half past nine the throbbing hurt was back. The other thing I didn't like about it was that it made me feel fuzzy in the head, as if I'd swallowed two pints of whiskey this afternoon instead. Must've had some alcohol in it along with laudanum or opium or whatever the hell else it was made out of.

That gawdamn quack dentist. Painless, my ass. He done yanked my broke tooth so hard it felt like part of my jawbone come out with it, then he wouldn't give me a free bottle of his pain medicine. Like I told Jennison, and Doc Christmas and that tub of lard works with him, a free tooth yank damn well oughta entitle a man to a free bottle, too, and that went double when the yank kept on hurting like billy bejesus for two days now. My jaw was still swole up so big I couldn't hardly chew solid food. All I'd had to eat was hardboiled eggs and bread and I was hungry as hell for meat.

The throbbing got so bad I took a couple of swigs from the jug of forty-rod I keep in my room back of the shop, but all that did was make me feel fuzzier in the head and so mad I could hardly see straight. Gawdamn that quack! I wasn't about to stand for him treating me the way he done. Ain't nobody diddles Elrod Patch and gets away with it.

Long about ten o'clock I had another swig of whiskey, got my five-pound sledge out of the shop, and headed on over to the willow flat. I kept the sledge under my coat when I crossed Central, lest I run into Abner Dillard, the night deputy. But the only living thing I seen was a mongrel dog that come sniffing around and that I give a swift kick when it didn't get outen my way quick enough. Townspeople were all inside their houses, snugged up comfortable and pain-free in their beds, bellies full of their evening feed. Thinking about that, with my jaw aching fierce and my own belly rumbling from lack of food, made me even madder.

When I come to the flat, I took a tighter grip on the sledge handle and edged into the trees along the bank. Doc Christmas and that lard-butt Homer was gonna be sorry they ever come to Box Elder, and to hell with the consequences!

ABNER DILLARD

Night marshal is just about the best job a man could ask for in Box Elder. Not that that's my official title, night deputy is, but night marshal's got a nicer ring to it and that's how I think of myself in private. The job's such a good one on account of this is a real quiet town except after the spring and fall roundups when the waddies come in off the ranches with their pockets full of pay, looking to raise a little hell. And there ain't nearly as many now as there used to be. Once in a while I have to break up a fight or lock up somebody for being drunk in public or disturbing the peace, but most nights pass with nary a whisper of ferment. This looked at first to be another one like that, but it sure as hell didn't turn out that way.

I finished my last rounds just shy of midnight. Everything quiet and settled, as it almost always is of a Sunday night, Occidental House and all but a couple of Shantyville saloons closed early for lack of business. Nights like this are the beauty part of being night marshal; once I'm satisfied that everything's as it should be, I go back to the jailhouse for a long snooze until dawn. If any of the cells is occupied, I sleep tilted back in Seth Jennison's chair with my feet propped up on his rolltop desk. But if all four cells in the block are empty, as they were tonight, I just open one up, shuck off my boots, and make myself comfortable on the cot inside. Seth's particular about keeping clean cells and bug-free mattresses and blankets, so it's almost like sleeping in my bed at home.

I corked off right away tonight, but not for long. Somebody coming in and making a ruckus woke me up. I sat up quick, some disoriented the way a man is when he's woke up sudden, and rubbed my eyes clear—and my first thought was that maybe I was still asleep and having a bad dream about a giant scarecrow come to life.

The noisemaker was a tall drink of water wearing a black coat slung over a striped nightshirt, long chin whiskers pooched out and hair sticking up like straw, waggling a bull's-eye lantern in one hand and saying something garbled like he was speaking in a foreign tongue. But he was real enough, not any dream figment. I seen that as soon as I hoisted up off the cot and went out there where he was standing.

"You're not Marshal Jennison," he said.

"No, I ain't. I'm the night marsh . . . the night deputy, Abner Dillard. Who in tucket are you and what're you yammering about?"

"Where is the marshal?"

"In bed asleep where most folks ought to be." By then I was awake enough to recognize the scarecrow—Doc

Christmas, the painless dentist that come into town the day before. "What's the idea barging in here half dressed in the middle of the night?"

"I am here to report a shooting."

I could scarce believe my ears. What with the town ordinance against sidearms, we hadn't had gunplay in Box Elder in so long I couldn't recall the last time. "A shooting? You ain't wounded someplace, are you? I don't see any blood . . ."

"I am not the victim, fortunately."

"Well, then, who is?"

"Elrod Patch, the blacksmith."

"Patch! Who shot him?"

"I did. In self-defense, when he attacked me after attempting to murder my horses."

Hell, I thought, maybe I'm having a bad dream after all. I shook my head, blinked a few times. Doc Christmas was still standing there with his lantern, looking at me as though I might be a little soft in the head.

"Run that by me again," I said.

He did, in more or less the same words. Then he added some so that I commenced to get the gist of what happened. Seemed Patch had snuck down to where the Doc and his assistant, Homer, had their wagon, with the intention of killing one or both of their horses picketed nearby. Doc and this Homer woke up and run outside in time to stop him from using his sledgehammer on the horses.

"Either he was drunk or out of his mind," the doc finished

up, "because then he tried to attack me with the hammer. I had no choice but to shoot him down like the cur he was."

"You sure he's dead?"

"As a doornail."

"All right. Let's go have a look and make sure."

I got back into my boots and we hoofed it down to the willow flat, where the big fat guy, Homer, was waiting. Sure enough, Patch was sprawled out dead near where the two big bay horses was picketed, a bullet hole where his right eye used to be. In one hand was a five-pound sledge-hammer, just like Doc Christmas said. I leaned down and took a sniff of Patch's mouth. Who-ee! He smelled like he'd been fortifying himself with forty-rod, all right.

"You wait here, both of you," I said. "I'll go fetch the marshal."

Which I done straightaway, and kind of a hard duty it was. Seth hates to be woke up in the middle of the night, and a thing like this not only surprised him as much as it done me, it made him growl and grump all the more while he got dressed. On the way down to the willow flat he snapped at me, "I told you about Patch's threats, and to keep a sharp eye on Doc Christmas and Homer and their wagon."

"I did," I said, which was partly true anyhow. "Last time I checked down there at the flat, everything was quiet. And I didn't see hide nor hair of Patch anywhere."

"Damn fool. Patch, not you, Abner. He must've figured he couldn't get away with busting up Doc Christmas's wagon, but that he might with killing one or both of the horses."

"Like he done with Ben Coltrane's steeldust. Misdemeanor charge and a fine."

"Be just like him to think mean and stupid when he was liquored up." Seth grunted and spat into the dust. "Somebody had to get himself killed, better him than anybody else I can think of."

"Good riddance, eh, Marshal?"

"I didn't say that. And don't you say it, neither. Ain't right to be disrespectful of the dead, even a son of a bitch like Elrod Patch."

Seth looked at the wound in Patch's eye and sniffed his mouth the way I done. Then he made Doc Christmas and Homer repeat to him everything that'd happened, not once but twice. Then he took a close gander at the Doc's pistol, which I hadn't done.

"You know," he said, "guns ain't allowed in Box Elder."

"Surely I did not violate the ordinance by keeping my weapon stored inside the wagon?"

Seth chewed on that, and allowed as how he reckoned not. He sniffed the muzzle, then checked the loads. "One shot fired."

"One was all that was necessary."

"You must be pretty handy with a pistol to hit a man square in the eye on a dark night."

"I don't wish to brag, sir, but I am indeed something of a marksman."

"Uh-huh. You or Homer here take the time to light a lantern before you come out of the wagon?"

"There was no time for that," Doc Christmas said, "with the horses frightened and fussing as they were. There was only time enough for me to grab my pistol."

"And you say you hollered at Patch before you ventilated him?"

"I ordered him to cease and desist his foul intention, yes, sir. That was when he turned on me with the sledge-hammer upraised. Inasmuch as I had no desire to have my skull crushed, I had no recourse but to fire."

"Clear case of self-defense," I said.

"Looks that way," Seth agreed.

"Will I have to remain in Box Elder for an inquest, Marshal?" Doc Christmas asked him.

"You will if the county attorney requests one, but that don't seem likely under the circumstances. I'll wire my report to his office in the morning. Don't you be thinking of heading off until I get an answer."

"I won't. I certainly won't. Homer and I are respectful of the law, aren't we, Homer?"

"Sure are," Homer said. "Mighty respectful."

Seth sent me to wake up another citizen, the under-taker, Farley Dayne, but Farley was used to late-night pickup calls and he didn't mind. Matter of fact, he was downright eager when I told him the name of the deceased. We rode back down to the flat in his wagon, and it took three of us, Seth and Homer and me, to hoist Patch's heavy carcass into the bed. Seth and me rode back to the under-taking parlor with Farley and helped him unload. Then the marshal went back to bed, and after a while so did I.

I hadn't seen any other citizens out and about on any of my back-and-forths, walking or riding, but I knew from past experience how quick word of a happening got around in Box Elder. By sunup half the town would know about the shooting, and by sundown it'd be just about everybody in the basin. And I'd give odds that there wouldn't be a single mourner among 'em.

R. W. SATTERLEE

Give-a-Damn Jones was sitting on the nail-keg bench out front, doing something I had never seen a tramp printer do before—reading a book—when I came to open up the *Banner* office early Monday morning. Usually Dad was the one to open up, but he'd gone off to interview Marshal Jennison and Doc Christmas as soon as he received word of Elrod Patch's death. A shooting was major news in Box Elder, cause for excitement and a front-page story under a banner headline in the next issue.

I was pretty excited myself. "Boy, oh boy, we've sure got our work cut out for us today, Artemas."

"Oh? Why is that?"

"Haven't you heard what happened last night?"

"No. What happened?"

"The painless dentist, Doc Christmas, killed Elrod Patch. Shot him dead down where his wagon's parked on the flat."

Artemas's only reaction was a raised eyebrow. He slipped the book into his pocket—a real book, small and leather-bound, not a dime-novel thriller like you'd expect a roadster to read if he read anything at all—but I was too worked up to pay attention to the title. "The doc been arrested for it?" he asked.

"No. Evidently it was self-defense."

As we went inside I told him what I knew about it, which were just the bare facts Abner Dillard had come to the house to report to Dad. I must have sounded happy that Patch was gone because he said, "A man's death is no cause for rejoicing, R.W."

"Oh, I know that, and I'm not. It's just that nothing much happens in Box Elder and a killing is important news, 'specially when the victim is a man like Elrod Patch." I drew up the shades and turned the sign in the window around so that it read OPEN facing outward. "Anyhow, now that he's gone to his judgment, you won't have to worry about him anymore."

"I wasn't worrying about him. But I'll admit it's one less thing to think about."

When we were in the press section, I said, "Dad said to tell you to put the sale-price ad for Box Elder Feed and Grain at the top of page two in two columns, instead of the bottom of page one. Mr. Flowers won't like it, but reports on Doc Christmas's arrival and then the shooting, plus this week's editorial, will likely take up the entire front page."

"Right-hand or left-hand columns for the ad?"

"He didn't say. Left-hand, I guess."

Artemas put on his leather apron, lifted an empty form

onto the make-up table, settled himself on the tall printer's stool, and picked up his brass composing stick and setting rule.

I sat down at Dad's desk. My job this morning was to
write up the minutes of last Friday's town council meeting. Pretty dull work, but Dad said that if I wanted to be a
newspaperman, I had to learn to write every kind of story.
The only problem with that was, he gave most of the hum-
drum ones to me while he concentrated on his editorials
and important events. Another thing he was fond of saying was that if I did a good job on whatever copy I was
assigned to write, he would run it unedited. But that had
yet to happen and I wondered if it ever would. Will Satterlee was finicky when it came to the journalism that appeared in his paper; he never let anything I or anybody else
wrote stand without blue-penciling to his satisfaction.

I couldn't seem to get started on the town council story;
my mind was still abuzz with the news about Elrod Patch.
I sat back after a time, chewing on the eraser on my
pencil, and watched Artemas finish readying the front
page—setting the masthead and slugging the surrounding
white space with furniture—and then set the form aside.
He put another empty on the table and started on page
two with Mr. Flower's sale-price ad. He was the fastest
typographer we'd ever had, and I'd told him so more than
once. The first time he'd shrugged and said, "There are
plenty faster. You should have seen Charlie Weems and a
fellow named Hull in their prime. Put me to shame."

I had peppered him with questions about his trade and his travels, and he'd been patient with me, providing ready answers. I asked him another one now.

"Artemas, do you carry a weapon when you're on the road?"

He gave me a sharp look. "What makes you ask that?"

"Just curious. Seems to me a fellow might need one for protection sometimes."

"Sometimes."

"So you do carry one? I would if I were a roadster like you."

"But you're not."

"Someday I might be."

"If you're smart, you won't. I told you that before."

"You seem to like it just fine."

"You don't know me well enough to make that statement, R.W. Now put your mind on your work and let me get on with mine."

"But you haven't answered my question about a carrying a weapon—"

"No, and I'm not going to. My business, nobody else's."

I kept quiet after that. But my interest in the kind of life he led, the dangers he faced, was more than just idle curiosity. Prior to his coming, I had been uncertain about my future goals, whether following in Dad's footsteps, taking over the *Banner* when he decided to retire, was what I really wanted to do with my life. Listening to Artemas had started me thinking that maybe I ought to give itinerant hand-pegging a try before I settled down to newspapering or some other pursuit. It sure seemed like an exciting, daredevil life.

Artemas had discouraged me when I brought it up before. For one thing, he said, you had to work hard along the way to learn the finer points of the trade. And while his was a world of new vistas and adventure, the freedom it offered was balanced by hardships; most who tried to live as he did couldn't abide the loneliness and uncertainty, and quit sooner than later for tamer, settled pursuits. He himself had done some reporting here and there, and been told by a couple of editors that he showed promise, and one day he might just take up that line himself. But when I pressed him, he admitted it was more likely he would remain a tramp printer until he was too old and infirm to ride the rails and bear the other adversities a man encountered on the road. Chances were, he said with a shrug, he would die in a strange town and be buried without a marker in a potter's field grave.

Well, that had given me pause. Maybe I *wasn't* cut out for the kind of fiddle-foot life he led. I'd have to think long and hard before I made any decisions about having a fling at it.

I finally thought of a lead for the town council story and wrote it down. That got me started and the rest began to follow easily enough. I was about half done when the bell over the door tinkled and Dad came hurrying in.

He was all a-quiver, the way he gets when something or somebody like Colonel Greathouse upsets him or a rare big news story breaks. He tossed his derby at the hat tree and said to me, "Go sit at the other desk, R.W. I have work to do."

"What did you find out, Dad? Any new details about—"

"Don't bother me with questions now. Read my story when I've written it, it will contain all pertinent information. Artemas, slug a three-column head in sixty-point bold for next week's front page—**Elrod Patch Slain.** And a thirty-six bold subhead—**Blacksmith Shot by Traveling Dentist in Self-Defense.**"

"Right away, Mr. Satterlee."

Dad pulled a sheet of copy paper over in front of him and began to write. When he was in a creative frenzy like this, he wrote longhand almost as fast as Artemas could set type. I was just in the way here; I went out front and finished my dull-as-dishwater town-council-meeting story standing up at the counter. But I could feel Dad's excitement like electricity in the air. It made me wish I was the one writing what he was right now, and think that I probably was cut out to be a newspaper reporter and editor just like him.

JIM TARBEAUX

Most of Monday and Tuesday I spent looking for work.

Cattle and ranching were what I knew best, even though I was rusty after those five years in Deer Lodge, so I started with the small ranches near Keystone and then moved on to the few that were left on the other side of the river. A couple of the owners and hiring bosses were civil enough, the others wouldn't have anything to do with me. The civil ones had full summer crews, skeleton mostly because of the losses they'd suffered during the Big Die and the low beef prices that hindered the rebuilding of their herds. One said he might be hiring for the fall roundup, but that was weeks away and even then it wasn't likely I'd be picked over loose riders with a clean record. I was not too proud to turn down any other job that might have been offered—stablehand, handyman, cook's helper—but none was.

I drove back to Keystone Monday night in a bleak mood. I'd set out with hope and determination, encouraged by Mary Beth's love and unshakable faith, but the way the day had gone burned it out of me. I had to have some kind of job; I couldn't get back on my feet, start to rebuild Keystone, without one. Well, there was another way—Mary Beth had again urged me to let her arrange a small low-interest loan through the banker father of a friend of hers in Billings. But she'd have to cosign in order for me to get it, and I couldn't have that. Swallowing what's left of your pride is one thing, choking on it another.

On Tuesday morning, feeling grim, I headed out to where the nesters had their half-section tracts along both sides of the river and the creeks that fed it. I knew damn well they'd all be too poor to afford a part-time hired hand for wages, but I went anyway. Driving the buckboard rather than riding the chestnut, on the notion that an unarmed man in an old wagon would be less threatening than one on horseback.

Quite a few farms had been established, separated from one another by jackleg fences, and others were in the process of being built. My first reaction to the sight of men with hand- and horse-drawn plows tearing furrows in the grassland was anger. Pa had been a cattleman most of his life, and like so many others he'd grazed part of his herd out this way. I remembered how pristine the rolling prairie had been in those days; now it was all scarred and altered in the name of progress, maybe for the better in the long run but then again maybe not. You couldn't blame the surviving small ranchers, nor even Colonel Greathouse, for their dislike of sodbusters.

I stopped first at the farms that looked to have been there the longest and seemed as prosperous as could be hoped for in country like this—the ones with sod houses instead of mere shacks, and vegetable patches and chicken runs and newly planted fruit trees. The men were all wary of a stranger—I didn't give my name or say where I was from—driving a buckboard and asking for work. Several had rifles or shotguns close to hand, after the trouble they'd had with night riders. Scandinavians and Germans, most first-generation immigrants who spoke little English, or pretended they did. The only ones who didn't dismiss me in a few curt words were a German named Rheinmiller and his sons, but as reasonably polite as they were, providing me and the chestnut with drinks of water, they had neither the money nor the inclination to hire me.

The newcomers I avoided, figuring them to be even poorer—all except for a medium-young Norwegian in bib overalls working on a partially finished sod house. His wife was helping him, but she was clearly pregnant and unable to do much. The covered wagon they'd arrived in was parked nearby. The shack was some twelve feet wide by fifteen long, the finished walls formed of cut lengths of sod stacked like bricks and covered with tarpaper and wood siding with openings for door and windows, the roof fashioned of willow poles topped by layers of grass and sod. He was sweating heavily and stooped from the hard labor. I felt sorry for him, and in spite of myself I stopped and offered help for no more payment than a meal. He not only turned me down flat, he grabbed an old flintlock rifle propped against one of the finished walls and ordered me off his property. Unlike me, he wasn't ready to swallow his pride, might never be. Care for his kind or not, you had to respect such a man.

Another long, hot, wasted day. It was after five when I got back to Keystone—dejected, tired, hungry. The only option I had left now, besides taking Mary Beth up on her offer, was to hunt some kind of job in Box Elder. Tate Reynolds had been a friend of Pa's in the old days; maybe I could talk him into hiring me in some capacity, as a swamper if nothing else. But more likely not. I'd made a little trouble for him a couple of times when I'd had too much liquor in my wild kid days, and he'd been one of the jurymen who'd believed Cable's lies and brought in the guilty verdict. But I had to try. Reynolds first, then the rounds of the other merchants, hat in hand, little better than a beggar humbling himself in front of hostile eyes.

The one good thing that might come of all this job hunting, whether I could find one or not, was that it was bound to put a question in the minds of some: If I'd stolen Tom Kendall's fifty-four hundred dollars and hid it someplace, why was I after menial work? And why was I fixing to stay on at Keystone? Why didn't I just fetch the money and head off for parts unknown? Those questions might—*might*— convince a few people besides Mary Beth, Etta Lohrman, Will Satterlee, and Fred Benson that I was innocent after all. If I couldn't pry a confession out of Rufus Cable before he died, having at least some of my neighbors give me the benefit of the doubt would make rebuilding my life and my reputation some less troublesome.

I drove the buckboard into the barn, unhitched the chestnut, rubbed him down with a gunnysack, fed him some hay in his stall. Then I walked over to the house, thinking about supper, and opened the door. And stopped dead-still two steps inside, tensing up, staring.

A man stood spread-legged in front of the old horsehair sofa, his hat pulled down low, his face covered by a red bandana, a Colt six-gun aimed straight at my belly.

AL YANDLE

I couldn't stop thinking about that money Tarbeaux stole. More'n five thousand dollars, a damn fortune. I could keep on working for forty-and-found until I was too old and stove-up to sit a saddle and I'd never see anywheres near that much total, never mind in one lump.

The things a man could do with all those greenbacks! The places he could go, the fancy women he could have—women a whole lot better-looking than the saloon girls and two-dollar whores in Box Elder and Miles City. He could even buy himself a piece of land, if he was of a mind to, and start up a little spread of his own. Down in Wyoming in the Powder River country, say. I'd ridden line for an outfit down that way one fall, before I come up here to Montana, and I kind of wished I'd stayed. I still had a notion to go back down there again someday.

Had Tarbeaux got the money yet from wherever he hid or buried it? Could be he had, but then why was he still here? Getting ready to run off with Colonel Greathouse's daughter? Galled me as much as it did Kinch to think of a jailbird like him with that pretty, big-titted filly. But maybe he hadn't gone after the money yet. Biding his time. Either way, that five thousand was where Tarbeaux could get his hands on it quick any time he felt like it, and on account of he'd already served his time nobody could stop him unless they caught him with it.

Or unless somebody took it away from him.

What could he do about it if somebody did? Report his stolen money had been stole from him to the marshal or the county sheriff? Hell, no! He'd just have to take the loss and keep his mouth shut.

It got so I couldn't think about nothing else. Tuesday morning Kinch sent me and Collie Burns out to check the boundary fences separating Square G land from the sod-busters' tracts along Big Creek, see if the furriners had tore down any more of the ones we'd mended. You couldn't trust them boogers even after the lessons we'd taught 'em with the night rides. Colonel Greathouse's orders, them raids. He was a hard man when he was crossed, no question about that. But a mostly tolerable boss until that last roasting the newspaper editor Satterlee give him. He'd been a holy terror since then, storming around snarling at everybody like a trapped bear. Kinch and Burns had worked for him long enough to take the abuse in stride, but I was fed up with it and about ready to quit and move on.

Anyhow, Collie and me rode out there and didn't find any new breaks, but my mind wasn't on the job. We finished early and started back, but halfway there I couldn't fight the temptation no more. I told Burns I had a stomach complaint and needed to go into Box Elder to see the doc. He shrugged and said he'd tell Kinch. Soon as we split up and he was out of sight, I headed for the river. I found a place to ford it and rode straight to Tarbeaux's ranch.

I left my horse in the cottonwoods like Kinch and me done last week, crept up close enough for a look down into the ranch yard. There wasn't no sign of Tarbeaux or anybody else. I waited a few minutes, but the yard stayed empty. The barn doors was shut, so he wasn't in there. Had to be inside the house if he was there at all. I mounted up again, rode along the backside of the rise and around close behind the house where there was more cover. Then I made sure that orangey hair of mine was tucked up tight under my hat, tied my handkerchief over my face, drew my sidearm, and eased up and around to the front of the house.

Tarbeaux wasn't there, either. He'd of had to be deaf not to hear me banging loud on the door.

It wasn't locked. I went in and made a search for the money. I looked everywhere I could think of, in all four rooms—even poked around in the fireplace hunting for loose stones, which there wasn't none. If the money was in the house it was hid so I couldn't find it. I was so riled by the time I finished I kicked over a table, scattering a rack of pipes and some other stuff across the floor.

That was when I heard the wagon come rattling into the yard.

I went across for a quick gander through the front window, near turning my ankle when my boot heel come down on something that broke and skidded. Tarbeaux, alone on the seat of an old buckboard. He drove it into the barn, stayed in there must of been ten minutes. My mouth was dry as dust, my heart hammering hard, when he finally showed. I watched him walk across the yard until he got close enough so I could see he wasn't wearing a sidearm, then I backed up and put my Colt on him when he come through the door.

He stared at me a few seconds without moving. Surprised, but he didn't look scared. Then he swung his gaze around the torn-up room and his mouth got tight and his big hands balled into fists.

"Mister," he said, "whoever the hell you are, you're a damn fool. I don't have anything worth stealing."

"You got five thousand dollars." I hadn't said a word when I come here before with Kinch, so I didn't make no effort to disguise my voice.

"No, I haven't. I didn't steal that money."

"Won't do you no good to lie, Tarbeaux. You stole it, all right, and you got it hid somewhere. Not in here or I'd of found it. Where is it?"

He didn't answer me. He was looking down at something on the floor, and he took a step in that direction.

"Stand still!"

But he didn't. Took another step and leaned down and picked up what he'd been looking at. Hell, it was nothing but a tintype of a woman in a wood frame that must've been setting on the table I'd kicked over. It was what I'd near tripped on going to the window, the frame splintered and the picture torn up some. He put the tintype into his pocket.

"Quit stalling," I said. "Where's the money?"

"Gone. Long spent by the man who did steal it."

"Bullshit. You're gonna tell or show me where it is, or else—"

"Or else what? You'll shoot me?"

"Better believe it."

"Gun hand of yours doesn't seem too steady."

He was right, it wasn't. I'd never drawn down on a man before, not like this, and the thought of having to pull trigger on him scared me a little. More scared than he was, the way he looked and talked. But I was in too deep now, I had to see this all the way through.

"It's steady enough," I said. "Better believe that, too."

"How do you figure killing me will get you the money?"

"I'll kill you slow, that's how. Bullet in the knee hurts like hell. You don't tell then, I'll blow out your other knee."

That convinced him, by Christ. He sighed heavy and said, "All right, mister, you win. I'll take you to the money."

"Where?"

"In the barn. Under a floorboard in one of the stalls."

"That better be the truth."

"It is."

"Move out, then. No more wasted time."

Tarbeaux turned for the door. It was still partway open, and he pushed it wider and stepped on through, slow. The thought of the money was so hot in my head that I followed him too close, didn't see he still had his hand on the door edge until it was too late. He flung the door back in my face the second he stepped outside. I tried to stop and dodge, but I had the Colt out in front of me and the door smacked into it and knocked it out of my hand.

Soon as Tarbeaux heard the gun hit the floor, he come back through raging like a bull and slammed into me and knocked me off my feet. I hit the floor on my ass, skidded backward into the couch. He jumped and landed on my chest with both knees, tearing the air out of my lungs and choking off a yell. I couldn't roll him off, couldn't hardly breathe, couldn't stop him from ripping the handkerchief off.

"Oh, so it's you," he said, and hit me in the face. I felt my lip split, my nose break and spurt blood. I was all over pain then, half blind and more scared than I'd ever been before. He hit me twice more, then lifted off. My eyes were too full of sweat and blood to see what he was doing, but I didn't have to—I knew he was after the Colt and that he'd get it before I could move.

I was all through. I knew that, too.

Crazy thing was, laying there hurting, gasping for breath, knowing I was a damn fool just like Tarbeaux said, I still couldn't stop thinking about the money.

COLONEL ELIJAH GREATHOUSE

I have had cause to hate many men in my life. Confederate snipers and backshooters during the war, cowards and insubordinates among the troops under my command. Rustlers, Indians. The sawbones in Billings who couldn't save Gloria when her female complaint turned life-threatening. The greedy speculators who'd overstocked the ranges before the Great Die-Up. The immigrant sodbusters ravaging the land like hordes of locusts. That no-account thief Tarbeaux still bent on turning Mary Beth's head.

But I have never hated any man quite so much or in quite the same way as I did that goddamned scourge of an editor, Will Satterlee.

He had been a burr under my saddle for a long time, too long. Attacking me every chance, spitting in my face in print, tearing down my good name—hell-bent on turning everybody in the basin against me. That last editorial of his vilifying me and defending Tarbeaux was the final straw. Every time I thought about it the rage flared up all over again.

Tarbeaux I would deal with later. I had given Mary Beth a tongue-lashing when Kinch and Yandle brought her back from Keystone, warned her she better not set foot on that jailbird's land or see him anywhere else again. Far as I knew she hadn't taken it into her head to disobey me. Should I ever find out she had, both of them would pay the price. She wasn't too old for me to take a willow switch to. And if Tarbeaux figured on sticking in the basin, it wouldn't be for long—I'd burn him out if I had to.

Satterlee was another matter. One that had to be dealt with now, before he did me any more damage. No man can do what he'd done to me in print, talk down to me the way he had last week, and get away with it. I couldn't live with myself if I let that happen. I am not a violent man by nature—all the killing I'd done had been justified in the name of the Union, or out of necessity to preserve what was rightfully mine—but in the old lawless days I would have found a way to prod Satterlee into a gunfight and then blown his goddamned head off. Now . . . no. The Territory, the whole country, was too tame, too law-conscious for that kind of retribution.

There was another way to teach Satterlee a lesson, warn him to back off or suffer worse consequences. I did not much care for the idea of it, but when a man gets pushed into a corner he fights his way out any way he can, with any method at his disposal.

Kinch had been around most of the day, supervising repairs on the corral fences, but I waited until late afternoon before I sent for him. I did not want him thinking too long and hard about what I wanted him to do. He had balked at first when I ordered him to show the goddamned sodbusters they couldn't get away with rustling and slaughtering Square G cows, but I made it plain I would fire him if he refused to lead the night raids, and he went ahead and led them. He'd do this, too.

I had him come into my study and close the door. Then, short and direct, I laid out for him what I had in mind.

He chewed his lip, rolling his Stetson around in his fingers. "I dunno, Colonel. You sure it's a wise idea?"

"Don't try to tell me what's wise and what isn't."

"No, sir. It's just that . . . well . . ."

"Well what?" I said. "Afraid of getting caught? You won't be if you're careful and do it after midnight."

"The noise . . ."

"Damn the noise. Nobody will be awake to hear it, including that stupid lazy night deputy. Besides, it won't take you more than a few minutes."

"Satterlee's gonna know it was done on your orders."

"Of course he will. I want him to know. But he won't be able to prove it. Neither will the law. Even if by some off chance you should get caught, tell the marshal it was your idea."

"Then what happens to me?"

"Don't worry about that. I'd see to it you weren't prosecuted."

"Colonel, can't you send somebody else?"

"I don't trust anybody else. You're not going to turn me down, are you? You know what it means if you do."

Kinch was still reluctant, I could see it in his face, but he had the sense not to put up any more argument. "No, sir. I'll do it."

"I knew you would," I said. "Good man. Ride out after dark. If anybody in the bunkhouse asks where you're going, you've got a yen to visit Tillie Johnson's parlor house. Wait someplace outside of town until the time comes, make sure you're not seen. Report to me first thing tomorrow."

He nodded, still fiddling with his hat.

"One last thing, Jada."

"Yes, sir?"

"Do a proper job and you'll find a bonus in your next pay envelope."

When he'd gone, I lit a cheroot and sat back in my swivel chair, feeling easier in my mind than I had in days. My only regret was that I wouldn't be there to see the look on Satterlee's face come morning.

MARY BETH GREATHOUSE

I don't believe in eavesdropping any more than I do in spreading gossip, and I've never done so intentionally. Not until today, that is. And then only because of where I happened to be and what I happened to overhear.

The Colonel must have thought I was down at the stables, or inside the house someplace where voices wouldn't carry to me through the thick wooden walls. Either that, or in his dark state of mind he had no thoughts about me at all. In any case he must have opened his study window to let in the thin, late-afternoon breeze and left it open when Jada Kinch came in to see him. I was outside in the garden just beyond the window, tending to the row of scraggly rosebushes that I managed to keep alive and blooming by sheer force of will. I would have walked away if the Colonel's voice hadn't carried just enough so I could hear what he began telling Kinch he wanted him to do tonight. Then I stood still and kept on listening.

At first I couldn't believe my ears. But I suppose it

shouldn't have come as such a shock. I knew Colonel Elijah Greathouse's history better than anyone, how ruthless he could be when he felt he'd been unfairly wronged or wanted something badly enough. His inflexibility had cost him my love, and Mother's during the last years of her life, but until he tried to come between Jim and me I'd respected him. What respect I had left was now completely gone, destroyed by the trouble he'd made for the immigrant farmers, threatened to make for Jim, and was now conniving with Kinch to make for Mr. Satterlee. This was the worst thing he'd done yet. It was as if his judgment had become clouded, as if he were losing control of himself.

I kept on standing there after they finished talking and Kinch left. I didn't know what to do. If I went in and told the Colonel I'd overheard, it wouldn't change anything. He would refuse to listen to reason, as always when his mind was made up—he never listened to me about anything important anyway. Curse me for an eavesdropper, rant and rave about how justified he was. And lock me in my room, forcibly if I resisted.

Should I ride into Box Elder and tell Marshal Jennison what was planned for tonight? Or warn Mr. Satterlee, which amounted to the same thing? The Colonel would never forgive me, not that his approval mattered to me any longer. I might not love or respect him, but he was still my father; I didn't want to be the one to have him arrested and put in jail. Yet neither did I want Mr. Satterlee to suffer grievously at his hands.

I had to do *something*.

Jim, I thought then, he'll know what's best.

There was still plenty of time to ride to Keystone, and then to Box Elder to keep Kinch from carrying out his orders. I slipped quietly away from the house and down to the stable. Kitchi, our Blackfoot stableman, was forking hay into the stall feeders. I told him I was going for a ride, and he fetched Southwind for me. His brows lifted when he saw me pick up a Dakota ranch saddle instead of the sidesaddle, but he didn't say anything. When I had it cinched down and the bridle on, I walked Southwind out through the rear doors past the corral and the outbuildings. A couple of the hands saw me when I mounted and rode off, but that couldn't be helped. The Colonel would know soon enough I was gone, but he wouldn't have any idea where I'd gone or for what reason.

I rode cross-country to the river ford, then to Keystone, at a gallop. But when I got to the ranch, there was no sign of Jim or his chestnut gelding. That would have been upsetting enough, but what I found when I opened the door for a look inside the house was really disturbing. Something had happened here not long ago, something bad. Furniture had been knocked askew, small items littered the floor, and there were splotches of coagulated blood in front of the horsehair sofa.

The thought that Jim had been hurt filled me with dread. Where was he? Chasing someone? Gone to town to seek medical attention, or to fetch the marshal?

Was the Colonel responsible for this, too?

I mounted Southwind again and rode like the wind for Box Elder.

SAM BENSON

Most sodbusters don't have a pot to piss in or a
window to throw it out of, but every now and then
one of 'em'll surprise you. Like this young Scandahoovian,
Halvorsen, who showed up at the livery wanting to buy a
horse and a buckboard. He was a newcomer, just arrived
by covered wagon from Minnesota with his wife and relatives. The wagon belonged to the relatives, so all he had
was a few belongings and money in his jeans that he'd
saved up for the trip. Not a lot of money, but enough to buy
the buckboard and a "gude horse for plow, pull wagon,
ride."

I showed him what I had available and dickered with
him some—he was willing to spend just so much—and we
settled on a price for the blue-tick roan I'd rented to Jim
Tarbeaux and a buckboard that had seen better days but
would hold together well enough. We went inside to my office so I could write him a receipt, and on the way Halvorsen
spied the broke-down Mother Hubbard saddle I'd let the
tramp printer, Jones, leave with me. It was still lying where

I'd tossed it next to one of the stalls. Neither Robbie nor I had gotten around to moving it into the tack room.

"Saddle is for sale, Mr. Benson?"

It wasn't worth a tinker's damn, that Texas saddle, twenty-five years old if it was a day and all wore out. I hadn't wanted it and neither had Rufus Cable; I figured I'd just burn it if Jones didn't come back to claim it when he left town.

"Well, now," I said, "it don't rightly belong to me. I've got a couple of better ones of my own for sale."

I took Halvorsen into the tack room and showed him the saddles. He liked them all right, but the prices were too high for him and I couldn't afford to come down any. I could have sent him to Cable's shop—Cable had a stock of secondhand saddles for sale—but he wouldn't sell cheap, either. I was loath to direct business his way anyhow, him being an unsociable cuss.

When we went back along the runway, Halvorsen stopped and took another look at the Mother Hubbard. "This is saddle I like," he said, showing his ignorance. "You sure is not for sale?"

"Well . . ."

"I give you five dollars for it."

Could've knocked me over with a feather. But I covered up my surprise and said, "I reckon the owner would take five dollars for it, all right. No reason why he wouldn't, it's a fair price."

He grinned like he'd just put one over on me. "Is a deal, then?"

"Sure thing, Mr. Halvorsen. It's a deal."

When he drove off in the buckboard, the Mother Hubbard in the bed, I had me a chuckle. Halvorsen had put one over, all right—on himself. Good thing for Jones I'm an honest man; if I wasn't, I could keep the five dollars with him none the wiser, long as he didn't come back asking about the saddle.

I thought about taking the money down to the newspaper office and, if he wasn't there, leaving it with Will Satterlee or his son. But that seemed like a lot of trouble. Robbie lived in Shantyville and Ma Stinson's, where Jones was lodging, was more or less on Robbie's way home. I could give him the money . . . no, I couldn't. You can't trust Indians with cash that don't belong to 'em, not even half-breeds. But what I could do, and what I did, was tell Robbie to stop by Ma Stinson's and leave word that I'd sold the Mother Hubbard and Jones could come pick up his four dollars whenever he was of a mind to.

Four, not five. Hell, I was entitled to a dollar brokering fee, wasn't I?

WILL SATTERLEE

I was locking the door to the *Banner* office, about to head home for supper with R.W., when I spied Jim Tarbeaux and another man, a cowhand judging from the clothes he wore, trot up Central on horseback and turn on Lincoln toward the jailhouse. Jim held the reins to the other horse, and the cowboy appeared to have his hands bound behind his back. Neither of them paid any attention to the stares of the few citizens abroad.

I hurried downstreet after them. By the time I reached the jailhouse they had dismounted in front and gone inside. Seth was still on duty and Jim and his prisoner were facing him in front of his desk when I burst in. Prisoner the cowhand was, for his hands were tied with a piggin' string. Bruises and streaks of dried blood marked his sullen, weathered face.

Well, now. This was certainly a week for news!

Of the three, the only one to glance my way was Seth, with an expression of mild annoyance, but he knew better than to attempt to turn away Will Satterlee on the trail of a story. He returned his attention to Jim and the cowhand.

"What's this all about?" he asked Jim.

"Malicious mischief, destruction of property, attempted extortion at the point of a gun." Tarbeaux's lean countenance was set in lines of grim determination. Using two fingers, he dipped a Colt six-shooter from his coat pocket and laid it on the marshal's desk. "This gun. Likely he'd have shot me if I hadn't taken it away from him."

"Hell I would," the other man muttered.

"Where'd all this happen?"

Jim said, "Keystone. I was out hunting work all day and this yahoo was waiting for me in the house when I got back. Masked, gun aimed at my belly. He'd been there a while."

"Doing what?"

"Looking for that damned fifty-four hundred dollars—money I never stole, never had." Jim's voice was sharp, his manner truculent, as if he expected once again to be disbelieved.

There was no disbelief in me. This scruffy cowhand had obviously succumbed to the false claims and the lust for easy mammon—another insidious attempt to victimize Jim Tarbeaux. No wonder Tarbeaux was short-tempered and on the defensive.

"Seen you around a time or two, mister," Seth said to the prisoner, "but I don't know you. What's your name?"

"It's Yandle," Tarbeaux said, "Al Yandle. He works for the Square G."

Ah, I thought, the Square G. Wouldn't it be glorious

if Greathouse had put Yandle up to the attempt? Not that that was very likely, but the Colonel was certainly capable of any underhanded scheme to further his own ends. This business was news at any rate, but if he *was* involved . . .

"Your own idea to head to Keystone, was it?" Seth asked the prisoner.

"I never went to Keystone," Yandle said. "Tarbeaux's making the whole thing up. He jumped me on the road on my way into town."

The lie was obvious to me from the tone of the man's voice, the darting shift of his eyes. It was surely obvious to Seth, too, but all he said was, "Why would he do that?"

"How should I know? Ask him."

"I told you exactly what happened, Marshal," Jim said. "You can believe me or not."

"I take it you want to press charges."

"Damn right I do."

Yandle said, "You gonna take a jailbird's word over mine?"

"You want more proof?" Jim said to Seth. "Here, look at this."

He removed something else from his pocket, laid it beside the weapon. Seth studied it with narrowed eyes; I moved closer to do the same. It was a photograph that had been torn, crumpled, smudged with dirt—a tintype of Flora Tarbeaux.

"Would I do something like this to my mother's picture, Marshal? Not hardly. Yandle did it with his boot heel."

Seth gave the cowhand a dark look before saying to Jim, "Untie his hands. I'll put him where he won't do no more harm."

When Yandle's hands were free, Seth unlocked the door to the cell block and ushered him into a cell. From the doorway I watched him sit on the bunk and finger his battered face, wincing. "I need a doc. Bastard busted my nose."

"You're lucky I didn't cave in your skull," Jim said.

Seth said, "Enough of that kind of talk. I'll fetch the doc when we're done here, Yandle. You ain't that bad hurt."

In the office, with the cell-block door shut, he asked Jim to go over again what had taken place at Keystone. Then he had him sign a complaint form. Jim had lost his bitter defensiveness by then, mollified by the marshal's acceptance of his story and Seth's subsequent actions. He nodded to me on his way out, acknowledging my presence for the first time.

I said to Seth, "I'll talk to you later," and quickly followed Tarbeaux outside. He was untying his horse's reins from the hitchrail when I stepped up to him.

"Where to now, Jim?"

"Back home, where else?"

"Have supper with me at the hotel."

"Not hungry, thanks."

"Coffee or a drink, then. I'd like to ask you a few questions."

He hesitated. "You already heard me tell what happened today."

"Yes," I said, "but for my account in the *Banner* I would like more details, perhaps a quote or two. I intend to emphasize the fact that Al Yandle, whether he acted on his own or on Colonel Greathouse's instructions, was on a senseless errand."

A corner of Jim's mouth quirked in a wry half-smile. "In that case, Will, I'd be pleased to sit down with you."

He left his horse where it was and we walked back to Central and on down to the hotel. When we entered the crowded dining room, a few of those seated at table cast open or covert looks at Jim. He ignored them, as did I—all but one. Rufus Cable, seated alone at a corner table. Jim's gaze was on Cable all the way across to the last empty table, and when we sat down there he took a chair facing in Cable's direction.

The waitress, Molly Unger, set menus before us and I ordered two cups of coffee. Jim was still staring at Cable. At first, Cable returned the stare; then he moved his chair a little to one side, his eyes on the plate in front of him. But he was no longer eating, just poking his fork at whatever food was on it.

I said in a lowered voice, "Have you spoken to Cable yet, Jim?"

"Once."

"And the result?"

"No result. Not yet."

"Is what was said between you private?"

"Yes. Just between him and me."

"What do you intend to do?"

"Clear my name, like I told you before."

"How?"

"My business. Suppose we let it go at that, Will."

I didn't press him. To do so would have been a mistake. I ordered a light meal and he followed suit—he was plainly hungry—and I asked my questions and wrote down his answers in my notebook. It was his opinion that Al Yandle had acted entirely on his own, driven by greed, and that Colonel Greathouse had no knowledge of what had been done at Keystone. I tended to agree with him—reluctantly, to be sure. In all fairness I could not and would not even hint in my account of the incident that the Colonel was implicated.

Molly had just served our food when Cable stood from his table and left the room in a stiff-backed stride, not looking our way. Jim watched him out of sight before he picked up his fork and began to eat.

RUFUS CABLE

I have little appetite these days, and when Tarbeaux walked into the hotel dining room with Will Satterlee I lost all taste for food. But I wasn't unhappy to see him. On the contrary. Him being in town tonight might just have solved the problem I had been fretting about—how to get word to him that I wanted to see him alone after dark, without leaving traces or making him suspicious.

What was he doing with Satterlee? Providing more fodder for those damn editorials defending him and by inference damning me, probably. Had he told Satterlee about our meeting the other day, that I'd faced him with an empty shotgun in the hope that he'd put me out of my misery? False hope, and now I was glad it had been. The new plan I'd come up with would prolong my life for a while, not end it fast like the old one would have, and I'd have some peace before I wasted away. If the plan worked, it wouldn't make any difference what he told Satterlee. And it would work, it *had* to.

Tarbeaux kept staring knifepoints at me across the room, but that was all right because people at the other tables took notice and would remember. Testimony to back up my story when the time came. Still, I couldn't put up with it for long or it wouldn't look right. Instead of staring back, I kept my eyes on my plate for a time and then, as if he were making me nervous, I stood up quick, left four bits on the table to cover my bill, and hurried out.

But I didn't go far when I left the hotel, just up to the corner. I leaned against the side wall there, waiting. It was coming on dusk now and there weren't many people on the boardwalks, the street all but empty. I had a brief yearning for a cigar to help pass the time, but the way my lungs were I wouldn't dare have smoked one if I'd had it. Smoking affected my wind, set me to wheezing so bad at times I felt like I was suffocating, and after the last cigar I'd tried, a couple of weeks ago, I had coughed up flecks of blood. What I was fixing to do tonight, if I could get Tarbeaux alone, would be hell enough on my lungs.

The wait seemed long, but it couldn't have been more than twenty minutes before Tarbeaux and Satterlee came out of the hotel. They turned upstreet in my direction. I ducked farther back into the shadows until they passed, then followed them to the newspaper office. They shook hands, Satterlee turned to unlock the door, and Tarbeaux went on downstreet. Good! Now if I could just get to him with nobody else around. I already knew what I would say.

Satterlee lit a lamp in the *Banner* office. I could see light leaking around the shades over the door and window as I came near. But he didn't pull up either shade, so I passed without being seen. Tarbeaux cut diagonally across Central and turned onto Lincoln. A wagon rattled past, and I crossed over behind it. His horse was tied to the rail in front of the jailhouse; I reached the corner just as he mounted. If he turned in the other direction—

He didn't. He came my way, riding slow. The shadows were lengthening and there was nobody nearby on either Lincoln or Central when I stepped out and called his name, not too loud, as he drew abreast.

He reined up. "What do you want, Cable?"

"To talk to you."

"Go ahead and talk."

"Not here, not now."

"Why not? What's on your mind?"

"Seeing you in the hotel tonight, the way you were staring at me . . . I can't go on dreading the sight of you." I didn't have to fake the tremor in my voice. I could feel myself sweating. "I . . . I think maybe we can work something out."

"Such as what?"

"I don't know, something that will satisfy both of us—"

"The only thing that will satisfy me is your signed confession."

"Please, Tarbeaux. My shop in an hour, all right?"

"Why wait an hour?"

"I need time to calm down, settle my thoughts . . ."

He made a snorting sound. "Shore up your nerve with liquor."

This had gone on long enough. I said, "One hour," and turned and walked away from him on Lincoln without looking back. No need to fake the falter in my stride, either. I really did need that hour to shore up my nerve, though not with liquor. I had never been much of a drinking man.

I walked straight to the shop, lit the Argand lamp in the front room, then sat down on my work stool to catch my breath. I felt a little sick, more than a little scared, but I was pretty sure I could go through with it if Tarbeaux showed up. No, not pretty sure—I *would* go through with it. And he would come. How could he resist?

I hung on to that thought, waiting for the sick spell to pass. When it did, I went into the storeroom to finish making preparations.

HOMER ST. JOHN

Doc Christmas and me closed for business at six o'clock, tied down his dentist's chair and put away all the tools. The marshal had stopped by earlier to tell us he'd got a wire from the county attorney saying there wasn't no need for an inquest, just as he predicted, so we was free to leave Box Elder any time. Which Doc decided might as well be tomorrow morning. We'd done just about all the business there was to do, more in the past two days than the whole two weeks before we come here. Once word spread about the self-defense shooting, folks flocked to the wagon to get a look at the gent who'd rid the community of that canker sore of a blacksmith. And plenty of 'em stayed to partake of the doc's services.

He was in fine fettle tonight, smiling and humming to himself, happy as a pup with two tails. And well he should be after three more extractions, four gold fillings, ten mouth examinations, an order for one complete set of vulcanite dentures, and every last bottle we had of Doc Christmas's Wonder Painkiller sold. Before we left Box Elder and went to another town, we'd have to buy some of the ingredients we needed to mix us up a new batch. Which we'd do in private somewheres along the trail in whichever direction the doc reckoned on heading. If we kept on doing this kind of business, we'd run out of gold and the other stuff Doc used sooner than expected; then we'd have to lay over in one of the bigger towns while we waited for his sublet dentist in Spokane to send us what was needed.

It'd been a real successful two days, all right, just as he figured it would be, but I still didn't feel right about the whole business. Lying to the law and deceiving folks the way we done. It was some sinful, even in a good cause.

The doc a marksman? Hell's bells, he couldn't hit the side of a barn with that old Colt pistol of his in broad daylight, much less shoot a man's eye out on a dark night.

He wasn't the one ventilated Elrod Patch.

The tramp printer, Artemas Jones, done it.

The way it actual happened, Doc and me was tucked up on our bunks and he was snoring away when the horses commenced to kick up a fuss. I was just barely dozing so I heard 'em plain and I knowed right away something was wrong. I shook Doc awake, then there was a yell outside, and just as I flung open the rear door I heard "Let go that hammer, Patch!" and a snarled answer I couldn't make out. I scrambled out of the wagon with Doc right behind me cussing, something he don't usually do.

Sure enough, the two of 'em was over by the horses, Patch with that five-pound sledge lifted straight up in the air and Jones about ten paces away with his legs spread and one arm stretched out long. "I'm warning you, Patch, I'll fire!" he yells, but Patch didn't pay no attention. He let out a bellow and charged. It was too dark to see the pistol in Jones's hand until it spit flame, surprising hell out of both Doc and me. And down Patch went like an axed steer.

The two of us run over there. Jones lowered his pistol and says half angry, half sad, "I had to do it. He didn't give me a choice."

"Self-defense," Doc says. Wasn't no doubt in either of us that that's what it was.

"He was getting ready to bash one or both of your horses," Jones says, leaning down to tuck the pistol into the top of his boot. "Would have if I hadn't come along when I did."

"We're grateful to you for stepping in. Why did you?"

"One of the things I can't abide is cruelty to animals."

"Us neither," I says. "Sure glad you stayed out walking long as you did."

"And that you were in the right place at the right time," Doc agrees.

"Just my luck," Jones says, which seemed like kind of a funny thing to say since the luck was all Doc's and mine.

Nobody'd been close enough to hear the shot, the hour being late and the flat being some distance from the nearest buildings. We got the horses calmed down, then Doc sent me to get a lantern out of the wagon and he looked close at Patch to make sure he was dead. Jones says he guessed he'd better go fetch the law, but he didn't sound happy about it. I asked him why and he says even with two witnesses to the fact he'd shot in self-defense, it was common knowledge him and Patch had had some trouble, and besides, the horses wasn't his property and he'd had no good reason to be walking around out here after dark. Likely the marshal would lock him up until an inquest could be convened, and maybe he'd be exonerated and maybe he wouldn't. Folks in small towns was always some leery of tramp printers in general, he says, and he'd figured to hit the road after the next issue of the newspaper come out.

That was when Doc had his brainstorm. "You did me a great service tonight, sir," he says to Jones, "now I propose to do you one in return. I shall be the one to lay claim to the self-defense shooting, otherwise telling the tale exactly as it happened. The horses are my property, and I have every right to defend myself when they and I are attacked. Patch threatened Homer and me and my belongings in front of witnesses, a fact which I reported to Marshal Jennison. Traveling dentists being less undesirable than traveling typographers, chances are I will not be held in custody or otherwise prevented from leaving Box Elder."

Jones didn't much like the idea and says so, but Doc talked him into it. Two things made up his mind for him, if you ask me. One was that ordinance against carrying guns in the town limits; he didn't have good reason to've kept his tucked inside his boot instead of turning it in at the marshal's office. The other thing was just before Doc finished his closing argument, a train whistle sounded off in the distance. Ain't no roadster I ever heard of could resist that call for long—it was like being pulled by invisible strings. He'd do whatever it took to keep from being tied down when the pull become too strong.

I knew Doc's suggestion wasn't all out of the goodness of his heart, that he had what he called an ulterior motive. He says to me later that Patch being a pariah, folks hereabouts would be relieved he wouldn't be around to bully 'em no more, hail Doc as a hero for ventilating him, and come around to show their appreciation. Which is just what they done. Doc may be a queer old bird, but he's whipsmart and always on the lookout for ways to feather his nest.

Anyhow, Jones finally give in. But before he left he says that if the law give Doc any grief, he'd go see the marshal and set things straight. He's got his own principles, too, Jones has. Meanwhile, Doc says, he wasn't to have any contact with us or us with him. Jones agreed to that, too, and kept to his word.

When he was gone, Doc got that old pistol of his out of the wagon, wrapped a piece of cloth around it, and went and fired a round into the river. Then he put on his coat, told me what to say when he come back with the law, and headed off for the marshal's office. I fretted some while he was gone, but it all come off slick as butter, just the way he said it would. Still, I hadn't been easy in my mind since, even after the marshal's visit this afternoon, and wouldn't be until we were long gone from Box Elder . . .

"Homer."

"Eh?"

"You were woolgathering. Why?"

"Oh," I says, "just thinking about getting back on the road again and all the work ahead of us." A little white lie. Wasn't no sense in sharing my misgivings with him. "I'll start the fire for supper—"

"No, not tonight, my boy," Doc says. "Tonight we shall celebrate with a restaurant meal in town."

"You sure that's a good idea?"

"And why not? We can certainly afford it, and we'll be well received. No one will bother the wagon or the horses while we're gone."

"If you say so."

"Lock up and we'll be off," he says, rubbing his hands together. "I haven't been this hungry for a rare beefsteak since we left Spokane."

SETH JENNISON

Sometimes, seems like, trouble comes in bunches like wormy apples.

You take all that had happened here lately. First the wrangle between Colonel Greathouse and the nesters, then Jim Tarbeaux coming back after five years in prison to stir things up, then Elrod Patch making threats and getting himself shot while trying to brain Doc Christmas's horses, then that Square G hand Yandle busting up Tarbeaux's place and demanding the Kendall loot at gunpoint. And now, just as I was sitting down to my supper at the Elite Café, here come Mary Beth Greathouse with yet another wormy apple for the barrel.

She headed for my table soon as she spied me. My office had been her first stop, she said, and Abner had told her where I was. She'd just come from Tarbeaux's place, and when she started in telling me what she found there, I said I already knew about it and explained how Tarbeaux had brought Yandle in and what had happened between the two of 'em. The fact that Tarbeaux was all right relieved her considerable. She wanted to know where he was now, and I said I didn't know, last I'd seen him was when him and Will Satterlee left my office together.

"How long ago was that, Marshal?"

"Must've been more'n an hour."

"Did they say where they were going?"

"No. Newspaper office, maybe. Might be Tarbeaux's on his way home by now."

"No, I'd have seen him on the road. He must still be in town." She nibbled on her lower lip, and a pretty one it was. Even a confirmed bachelor like me never gets too old to admire an attractive girl and her assets. "I should try to find him before I tell you what else happened today, but now that I'm here ... I better not hold it back any longer."

"Hold what back, Mary Beth?"

"I guess you know how upset the Colonel has been over Mr. Satterlee's last editorial. This afternoon I overheard him ordering Jada Kinch to ... well, to see to it that there wouldn't be another one for a good long while."

"See to it how?"

"By breaking into the *Banner* office tonight and doing as much damage as he could to the printing equipment."

There it was, the latest trouble, the apple with the worm wiggling around inside. Hellfire! The Colonel must've taken leave of his senses to issue a fool order like that, and Kinch likewise to agree to carry it out. But I didn't say that to Mary Beth. She was wrought up enough as it was.

I patted her hand and said, "You done the right thing, telling me. What time is the break-in planned for?"

"They didn't say exactly. After midnight sometime. The Colonel told Kinch to ride in after dark, but to stay out of town until it was time. What are you going to do, Marshal?"

That was a good question. Didn't matter where Kinch was now; even if I could find him, I couldn't arrest him on hearsay evidence before he committed a crime, and he'd just stonewall me anyway. Besides which, I couldn't very well tell him how I'd found out. But neither could I let him vandalize the newspaper office. The thing to do, then, was to set up watch and catch him in the act of breaking and entering. He wouldn't be stupid enough to come in the front way, so the place for a watch was in the back alley within sight of the rear door.

I sure didn't relish the idea of standing around for the Lord knew how long waiting for Kinch to make his move, tired as I was after a long day. I could give the job to Abner, but he's got his rounds to make and he's a lazy cuss, sleeps more hours than he's awake—not the most reliable deputy I've ever had. Nor the bravest. Kinch is big and knot-tough. Hell, he'd eat Abner for breakfast.

No, like it or not, the job was mine.

I said to Mary Beth, "You just leave things to me. I'll see to it Kinch don't do what he was told to."

"What about the Colonel? Will you have to arrest him?"

"Not me, the Square G's out of my jurisdiction, but I reckon the county sheriff will when I report to him. Inciting illegal trespass and destruction of private property is a felony crime."

She gnawed on her lip some more. "He'll go to prison?"

"Jail yes, until he posts bond. Prison . . . I reckon not, if there's no actual destruction. Judge will most likely slap him with a big fine and put him on probation."

"Would I have to testify against him?"

"You would if Kinch don't own up. You're the only other witness."

"I don't know if I can do that. My own father . . ."

Well, she wouldn't have a choice if there was a trial. And there would be; Will Satterlee would make certain of that. I could just see him licking his chops when he found out about this. And he would—no way to keep it a secret.

But I didn't say any of that to the girl. "Let's not get ahead of ourselves, Mary Beth. Important thing right now is for me to put a stop to this foolishness before it gets out of hand. Might be a good idea for you to take a room at the hotel for the night. Kind of late to be riding all the way back home alone."

She got up on her feet. "Not until I find Jim," she said, and hurried on out with her back straight as a stick. She had her head screwed on the right way and plenty of sand, but I felt sorry for her just the same. Hadn't been easy coming to me the way she had, in defiance of a stubborn, reckless old grudge-holder like Colonel Elijah Greathouse. I wouldn't put it past him to disown her for what he'd consider disloyalty.

I had my supper, without enjoying it much, and then went to find Abner and tell him about the latest wormy apple.

JIM TARBEAUX

I didn't trust Cable or his motives. A sudden change of heart wasn't like him at all. Possible, maybe, but more likely he had something up his sleeve. But what? Not meeting me with his shotgun loaded this time. He was a coward clean through; I doubted he had the guts to pull trigger on me from ambush, much less look me in the eye. Why the hour delay, then? And why the saddle shop?

Well, I'd find out soon enough. And after what had happened with that bastard Yandle this afternoon, I would be extra careful. Even though I wasn't worried about being met with violence, I wished I had a sidearm that I could conceal under my coat just in case. As it was, I would have to trust my ability to handle the situation unarmed. I couldn't very well walk into the shop toting the old Springfield and risk spooking him if Cable really was ready to come clean.

To kill an hour, I rode over the bridge to the schoolhouse in its cottonwood motte. I could have stayed in town, had a glass of beer at the Occidental or something to eat at the café, but that would've meant being stared at, whispered about. I'd had enough of that. The time would come when I could do as I pleased in Box Elder, no longer an object of scorn and distrust, but that time was still a long way off.

I went to the schoolhouse because it was deserted at night, a good place to sit quiet and wait, and because I had a small nostalgic feel for it. Most kids resented time spent learning their ABCs, but I hadn't. I liked reading books, finding out new things—it had made cell time in Deer Lodge a little easier to get through—and I'd even liked the teacher, a stern but fair spinster lady, Miss Seeley, who'd long since died. But I hadn't learned my lessons well enough back then. If I had, I'd have been able to control that streak of wildness, never chased around with Bob Kendall, never touched that fifty-four hundred dollars.

I ground-hitched the chestnut and walked around the schoolhouse, looked in through one of the windows even though I couldn't see much in the darkness. Then I sat on one of the benches and rolled a cigarette and tried not to fidget. A breeze had sprung up, making the night cooler than the last few. It was almost pleasant sitting there, smoking, a free man looking up at the bright clusters of stars in the big Montana sky. Almost.

Without a watch I had to rely on instinct to tell me when the hour was near up. If I was a little early, so what? I mounted and rode back into town, onto Territory Street to Cable's saddle shop. The shade was partway up on the front window and lamplight glowed inside. The door wasn't locked; I opened it far enough to scan the main room without entering.

Cable wasn't there. But when I called his name, he answered from behind a partly open door across the room. "You alone, Tarbeaux?"

"I'm alone."

"Come in, then. I'll be right with you."

I stepped in, shut the door after me, and went a little way toward Cable's workbench. Funny. It seemed emptier than it had before, some of the tools gone. The rest of the room, too, fewer examples of his trade on display. Why would he have moved all of that out?

The odors of leather and harness oil were as strong as before, but the smell of something else was mixed in with them now. Not in this room, somewhere behind that partly open door. It took only a couple of seconds to identify it.

Kerosene.

In the next second I heard the slamming of a door and then a sudden loud *whoosh!* Spears of yellow-orange flame and a coil of black smoke came shooting through from the rear. The sudden heat was like a furnace door being thrown open.

The son of a bitch had set fire to his own shop!

I spun toward the front door. Cable must have put some sort of accelerant on the floor in here, too; the fire licked at my heels as I yanked the door open, flung myself through, threw it shut again behind me. A man was coming along the boardwalk a short distance away; he yelled something at me that I didn't pay heed to. There was an alley between the saddle shop and a carpentry shop next door and I veered into it. Before I reached the end, another man came running past in the cross alley behind the shop. Starshine and fireglow let me see that he wasn't Cable, a man I didn't recognize. He either saw or heard me, shouted "Fire!" and kept on going.

I ran the opposite way, the way he'd come. The entire back wall of the saddle shop was ablaze, flames already eating at the shingled roof, oily black smoke billowing high into the clear sky. I felt the singeing heat as I dodged by, raced up the alley to the next corner.

There was no sign of Cable anywhere.

WILL SATTERLEE

I had just finished writing a long account of Jim Tarbeaux's run-in with Al Yandle when the commotion started. Shouts rose out on Central, followed by the sudden loud ringing of the bell mounted on the wall of the Volunteer Fire Brigade. There was no mistaking that sound. And when the bell began clamoring as it was now, loud and steady with no pauses, it meant that a fire of some size and danger had broken out within the town limits.

I blew out my desk lamp and hurried outside. Several men summoned by the alarm were scurrying along the boardwalks and in the street, heading down toward the river; others spilling out of the Occidental House across Central increased their numbers. The blaze appeared to be three blocks distant, its smoky, pulsing glow lighting up the sky. Sight of it dried my mouth, put a tightness in my chest. Judging by the amount of firelight and smoke, at least one building was ablaze and possibly more.

I joined those racing downstreet. Some of the running men angled off to the west, volunteers heading for the firehouse on the riverbank near the old steamer landing. If it weren't for my age and heart murmur, I would have been one of them. The babel of voices and racket from the fire bell built echo after echo until the night itself seemed to have come alive.

The burning building was on Territory Street east. As I reached the intersection, I heard someone who was already there cry out, "It's Cable's saddle shop. Christ, if he was in there he's burned to a crisp."

I ran out to where I had a better view. The saddlery was sheeted with flame. And already there were spots of fire licking along the walls and on the roofs of the two adjacent buildings, Pete Noonan's carpentry shop and O'Hearn's barbershop on the corner. Cable's place was burning hot and fast, the way a summer-dry wood structure will. Sparks and embers flecked the smoke that laid a widening black pall over the sky. Firelight bathed the street in a ruddy glow that glinted off window glass, made blackened silhouettes of the swarming, bunching citizens.

A ragged bucket brigade was in progress in an attempt to save Noonan's and O'Hearn's until the volunteers arrived, the water coming from horse troughs and fire barrels, but it was having little effect. There was a vacant lot on the far side of the carpentry shop; not too much danger in that direction. But if O'Hearn's blazed up and touched off the milliner's shop next door on Central, the entire block was liable to burn like dry tinder in a stove. I had seen it happen once before, in Laramie eight years ago; five buildings and two men had died in that conflagration.

This one could turn out to be a devil of a lot worse. Should the fire spread to Flowers Feed and Grain down at the end of the block, and then jump the intersection to the hotel, it would burn the heart right out of Box Elder.

There was nothing I could do here. I ran on down to the river to see if I could be of any help to the volunteers. By the time I reached the firehouse, half a dozen men had the engine cart out and were filling the hub tank with a suction hose dipped in the adjacent cistern. Once it was full, they began dragging the cart, axles squealing, along the street; others young and strong joined them to help make haste. There was nothing I could do here, either.

The man working the fire bell was Glen Randle, the Western Union operator. I shouted at him, "Any idea how the fire started, Glen?"

"Might've been set on purpose," he shouted back.

"What? What makes you think that?"

"Ask Bert Lawless if you can find him. He's the one come and got me. Said he saw that ex-con Tarbeaux running out of the saddle shop just after it blazed up."

"Tarbeaux? Is Bert sure?"

"Said he was."

I had difficulty believing it. Tarbeaux had been adamant about clearing his name and doing it through non-violent means. Had he lied to me, and revenge was his primary motive all along? But I had difficulty believing that, too. I pride myself on my judgment of a man's character and I know instinctively when I am being lied to. I had had no such feeling of deceit when I spoke to Jim Tar-beaux.

I followed the volunteers back to Territory Street. Noonan's and O'Hearn's were covered in flames now, too. The heat was intense, thrumming and crackling. Embers danced out of the flame-edged smoke; a pine knot as big as a baseball exploded from the saddle shop and just missed arcing all the way across the barbershop. Had it landed on the tar-paper roof of the milliner's and set that building ablaze, the next two in line would have followed suit and likely doomed the feed and grain store as well.

Seth Jennison and Abner Dillard were there, yelling for people to stand clear so the volunteers could unreel the hundred feet of one-and-a-half-inch cotton hose. So was Rufus Cable, trying and failing to convince Seth to listen to what he was shouting. He moved back, swinging his gaze left and right, and when he saw me he came running.

"Tarbeaux!" he shouted, as if the name were an obscenity. His eyes bulged big as half-dollars in his sweat-sheened face. "Tarbeaux did this!"

"How do you know that?"

The smoke was affecting his lungs; he spewed words through a series of hacking coughs. "I saw him, Will . . . saw him spill kerosene in the storeroom and light a match. He knew . . . knew I was working late. Tried to kill me . . . burn me alive . . ."

Two witnesses now, yet I still had difficulty believing Tarbeaux as an arsonist and would-be murderer. Cable might be attempting to frame him again, as he had five years ago. Bert Lawless was a credible witness, but he could have been mistaken. Still, there was little doubt that the fire had been deliberately set. Kerosene, Cable had said. The pouring smoke carried the oily appearance and unmistakable odor of it.

Cable kept babbling at me, tugging at my arm. I stepped away from him, my attention on the volunteers. They had the hose hooked up to the pump now. With half a dozen men manning the cart brakes, the engine was capable of producing a flow of some forty gallons of water per minute. Little enough with a fire this size, but enough, God willing, to save the rest of the block.

Arlo Phipps, the volunteer fire chief, was up on the cart handling the pump and cussing. I was close enough to hear him yell, "Damn thing don't want to work right. I told the town council we needed new equipment, I *told* them . . ."

A sharp rattling noise came from the pump and ended his complaint. One of the other men said unnecessarily, "She's ready now, Arlo."

"About damn time. Soak the milliner's and the buildings next to it. Nothing we can do about the three burning."

Two volunteers carried the brass nozzle while others laid the hose out in a line behind to lessen weight and side-pull once the water flow started. When they were ready, one of them signaled back to Arlo to start the pump. The hose and nozzle bucked like a wild horse; it took the nozzle men several seconds to maintain a steady stream.

It seemed as though the entire population of Box Elder had been drawn by the fire bell and the flames. Those that weren't helping fight the fire milled on Central and along the far sides of Territory Street. The heat from the three burning buildings was tremendous. It encased me in perspiration, gave my face a raw feel.

Cable had disappeared into the crowd. I looked for R.W.—he was bound to be here somewhere—but I couldn't locate him. Doc Christmas and his assistant were standing at a distance from the main body of watchers, as if afraid to get too close to the fire. Not far from them, at the outer edge of the crowd, I spotted Jim Tarbeaux. Mary Beth Greathouse was beside him, clinging to his arm; what she was doing in town at this time of night I couldn't imagine. I suppressed the newsman's urge to approach Tarbeaux, tell him what I had twice been told, gauge his reaction; this was neither the time nor the place. I would have to wait to talk to Bert Lawless, too, for he was one of the volunteers.

The milliner's tar-paper roof was smoldering now in two places and a little island of flame had risen toward the front. The hosemen managed to douse all three in time to keep the roof from catching fully. When they finished drenching it and the front of the building, they started in on the side wall of the hardware store.

Just as it looked as though the battle might be won, the pump pressure suddenly fell and the stream of water slackened off to a pizzle spurt. The hub tank was out of water.

There was no time to roll the cart to the cistern or the river; the volunteers frantically refilled with fire buckets from the brigade line.

Before there was enough water in the tank for the pump to work properly again, burning embers jumped the milliner's and touched off the hardware store roof. Seconds later the saddle shop's roof collapsed in a thunderous roar, a fountain of sparks and embers. One of the volunteers was struck by a flying section of roof beam and knocked flat. Liam O'Hearn. His clothing began to smolder as he struggled to free himself. The beam had fallen across one of his legs and had him pinned.

Seth Jennison got to him first, kicked at the beam fragment and sent it rolling off Liam's leg, then dropped down beside him, smothered the burning cloth of his trousers. The inferno's smoke and searing heat robbed both of them of breath, had them choking and half blind by the time others reached them and pulled them away. Poor Liam. As though losing his barbershop weren't injurious enough.

Helpless and angry, I watched the fires pulse out smoke and throw goblin shadows across the faces of the volunteers. Listened to the crackling heat, the snapping of timbers, the hiss and spit of water pouring out of the hose, the shouts and cries and curses. It was like a glimpse of the Pit, and it seemed to go on and on.

JADA KINCH

I was in a line of trees on the near side of the railroad tracks, a quarter of a mile from the Shantyville edge of town, when the fire bell started clanging. I hadn't been there long, maybe five minutes, and I was hunting for a patch of ground to spread my soogan for what I figured to be a long wait. That bell surprised hell out of me. It was loud enough to wake the dead.

I run out to where I had a clear look. The fire was on the lower end of the business district, but from this distance I couldn't tell exactly where. But the size of the glow and the amount of smoke pouring up and the way the bell kept clamoring made it a big one. Half the town would be headed for the blaze if they weren't already there; lamplight showed in all the shacks and saloons in Shantyville that I could see. Wasn't nobody I ever knew, unless he was drunk, crippled, or half dead, could stay clear of a fire that size no matter what time of day or night.

I had a notion to ride in there myself, find out what was happening. But that would've been stupid, letting myself be seen in town before I went and did what the Colonel wanted. Or would I be able to do it tonight? As hot as that fire looked, it was liable to spread and burn up a whole bunch of buildings, and there'd be townspeople out and around until dawn. Why not just ride back to the ranch, tell the Colonel that I'd had to call it off on account of the fire—

Yeah, sure, but all that'd do was postpone it to another night. He was hell-bent on getting even with Satterlee. Gone half loco in his old age, by Christ. Having the newspaper office busted up was a crazy idea. Even if Satterlee and the law couldn't prove nothing, they'd know the Colonel ordered it and I was the one done it and be all over me same as him.

But I *had* to go through with it. If I didn't, I might as well pack up and ride soon as I got back to the Square G, and where the hell would I go? Ramrodding jobs were scarce as hen's teeth these days, and I was getting too long in the tooth myself, too set in my ways, to give mine up— the only decent-paying one I was ever likely to have.

The fire bell kept on clamoring loud. I could see the flames now, the smoke spreading black as ink across the sky. And then another thought come to me. Whatever building or buildings was afire looked to be three or four blocks from the newspaper office. Wouldn't be anybody around there now. If I could get to it without being seen, wouldn't be any need to wait until after midnight to do the Colonel's half-assed bidding.

All right, then. Ride in careful and do it now, get it over

with quick, then head on out again while everybody was paying heed to the fire. Never be a better time, this night or any other.

I swung into leather and rode in at an angle past the outer cluster of Shantyville shacks, avoiding the lamplight as much as I could. Most of the businesses on the upper end of Central were dark and I didn't see anybody as I swung in a couple of streets below the railroad depot. The newspaper office was between Frontier and Powder, and there was a big box elder at the end of Frontier to mark the way.

I eased my pony in along there. But it would've made no never mind if I'd come in at a gallop—the racket from the bell and people shouting downstreet where the fire was covered any noise I made, and it was as deserted here as I'd figured it would be. The drifting smoke blotted the sky, but there was enough glow from the fire so I could see where I was going all right.

An alley ran behind the block between Frontier and Powder. I dismounted and ground-hitched my pony just inside it, went the rest of the way on foot. The newspaper office was halfway along, the widest building on the block, so I had no trouble finding it. Rear door was locked, but it wasn't much of a lock. Took me about half a minute to pry it open with my barlow knife.

Black as pitch inside, even with the alley door open. I pulled it shut and swiped a lucifer on my boot heel, held it up and moved it around to get the lay of the big printing room. Then I followed its smoky light across to where the cases of type and such were.

The match burned out just as I got there and I was back in darkness again. I'd seen oil lamps on the two desks in there. Light one, with the wick turned down low, so I could see what the hell I was doing? Better not. No need for it—I could get the job done well enough in the dark, fire a match when I needed one to point out the targets.

I yanked the heavy type trays down first, one after the other, slamming them into the floor. Metal slugs went bouncing and rolling every which way. Another match showed me a stone table and a stool and some other print-er's stuff. The table was heavy, but I got it thrown down. Then I smashed the stool, tore off one of its legs, and used it to sweep everything off one of the desks. I was making a hell of a lot of noise, but who'd hear it? Wouldn't carry far with all the racket outside.

When I had another match scratched and burning, I started toward the other desks. Only my foot slipped on the types scattered across the floor and I near lost my balance. Dammit to hell! I should've left the type trays for last. Now I'd have to light a lamp or else risk breaking a leg or my fool neck.

There was one in a wall bracket. I went over and lit it, my jammed knee sending up little shoots of pain, then lowered the wick until I had just enough light to see by. Then I got back to it, cussing the Colonel and myself under my breath the whole time.

DOC CHRISTMAS

Homer and I were in the hotel dining room, about to partake of our celebratory meal, when the fire bell commenced its furious summons. Naturally we were drawn outside along with everyone else, though as a rule I do not find conflagrations a source of either curiosity or fascination. As a matter of fact, I have an aversion to them stemming from my youth in Spokane, when I had the misfortune to witness a stable fire on a neighbor's property. To this day the screams of dying horses linger in my memory and now and then produce a disturbing nightmare.

Nonetheless we hurried outside, and when we located the source of the fire, I allowed Homer to tug me along in the rush of townsfolk. Most went as near the burning building as they could safely get, but once I saw the nature of the fire I stopped and refused to be drawn any closer.

"Looks like a bad one," Homer said.

"Indeed."

"Wonder what business it was."

A rhetorical question that neither had nor required an answer.

"What do you suppose started it?"

Another of the same.

"Sure hope nobody was inside when she went up."

"Indeed."

"Bound to spread and burn up the entire block if they don't get it under control pretty quick." Ever a man to state the obvious as well as the unanswerable, my erstwhile assistant. "You reckon there's anything I can do to help, Doc?"

"Hardly. You would only get in the way."

"Guess you're right."

We watched the volunteer firemen bring a pump engine and other equipment and set about their desperate work. Homer would no doubt have stayed for the duration of the battle, but the flames, the clamoring bell, the excited babel of voices, and the fact that I had had nothing to eat since breakfast combined to make me feel slightly nauseous. The thought of the destruction caused by rampant fire was unpleasant enough; witnessing it was literally painful.

"Enough of this," I said. "It's time to return to the wagon."

"You don't want to wait and see what happens?"

"I do not. Stay if you wish, Homer, but I am leaving."

He hesitated, but when I turned and walked away, he waddled up beside me. "Might as well go with you."

We were the only ones to leave the scene. A few latecomers passed us as we proceeded down Central Street, but by the time we crossed Frontier Street we were alone on the boardwalk. We were just passing by the newspaper office when Homer stopped abruptly.

"What was that?" he said.

"What was what?"

"A light just flickered inside, like somebody lit a match." He moved over to peer through the front window, the inside shade over which was partly raised.

"The estimable Mr. Satterlee, perhaps, about to light a lamp."

"No, sir. It went out and another ain't been struck."

Several seconds passed without a recurrent flicker. But then Homer said, "Hey! You hear that, Doc?"

"All I hear is the fire bell."

"No, I mean inside. Sounds like somebody's busting things up in there."

"A figment of your imagination."

"Uh-uh. You know I got twenty-twenty hearing. Listen!"

I stepped to the window beside him, pressed an ear against the glass. By gad, Homer was right. It *did* sound as though someone were wreaking havoc inside.

Homer put a hesitant hand on the latch. "You want me to go in and see what's up?" From the tone of his voice, he wanted my answer to be no.

I obliged him by saying, "I do not. We can't afford to become involved in what is likely a criminal matter."

"We got to do something—"

"And we shall. Or rather you shall. Run back down and inform Mr. Satterlee or Marshal Jennison. Quickly, Homer. Quickly!"

He set off in one of his waddling sprints, a ludicrous sight at the best of times. But despite his girth, he set a remarkably fast pace.

Inside, the crashing and banging ceased. I turned back to the window just as a match flared in the rear part of the office. To my surprise, whoever was in there lighted a lamp and turned the wick down low. The sounds and now shadowy visual images of wanton destruction commenced once more.

R. W. SATTERLEE

I couldn't seem to find Dad in the melee, but I did come upon Artemas Jones standing by himself on the southwest side of Central. Had he seen my father? I asked him.

"A little while ago. On Territory Street talking to Rufus Cable."

"So Mr. Cable wasn't in his shop when it caught fire. Whew! That's a relief."

Artemas didn't say anything. He was watching the volunteer firefighters trying to put out spots of fire along the far wall and on the roof of the hardware store. It looked to me that they would be able to save it. The saddle shop and Noonan's carpentry shop were glowing shells now, the barbershop and milliner's beyond saving, but if the volunteers saved the hardware store, the loss would be confined to just four buildings—something of a miracle with everything in Box Elder as summer-dry as it was.

"Jones! Hey . . . hey, Jones!"

We both turned to see Doc Christmas's assistant, Homer, come pelting up with his arms waving. He was het up about something, his fat face pouring sweat, his breath sawing in and out of his huge chest. "Somebody's in . . . inside the newspaper office. Doc and . . . Doc and me heard him busting things up in there. He sent me for help—"

Artemas didn't let him finish. He snapped to me, "R.W., go find the marshal," and took off running.

I probably should have done what he said, but what Homer had told us excited me more than the fire had, set my blood to bubbling hot. Without thinking I told Homer to fetch Marshal Jennison, and Dad if he could find him, and ran after Artemas.

I don't know whether he'd have yelled for me to go back if he'd seen or heard me, but he never once looked over his shoulder. He had a half-block lead and was fast on his feet, but I was younger and faster still. I was only about thirty yards behind him when he veered off onto Powder Street. I charged around the corner myself, just in time to see him disappearing into the alley that ran behind our shop. Whoever was doing the damage must have broken in through the rear door and that was where Artemas was bound, too.

The door was partway open, lamplight laying a feeble shine on the darkness, and I could hear the crashing, banging noises inside. He flung it wide and plunged through. The noises stopped and there was a yell, a curse, just as I reached the doorway.

I sucked in my breath when I looked inside, and not because I was winded from the run. The press room had been brutalized, all right, type trays and frames and forms and lamps smashed, furniture overturned or knocked askew, types and quadrats glinting all over the floor. And Artemas was grappling with the man who'd done it, their arms wrapped around each other like a couple of wrestlers, their bodies twisting this way and that among the wreckage. The feeble light came from the lamp in the wall bracket next to the press, about the only thing that hadn't been damaged, and when Artemas spun the man around I saw without much surprise who he was. Colonel Greathouse's foreman, Jada Kinch.

As angry as I was, I couldn't just stand by and watch; I ran in with the intention of making the struggle two against one. I took a fistful of Kinch's shirt and tried to jerk him loose, but the way he and Artemas were twisting around, I lost my grip and then my balance when one of Kinch's flailing arms struck me across the chest. I staggered backward, tripped over one of the broken trays, and fell sideways into the wall. My head hit hard enough to cockeye my vision for a few seconds. When I could see again, Artemas and Kinch had broken apart and Kinch was backing up and clutching at his holstered pistol.

Artemas went after him, stumbling, shouting at me, "Stay down, R.W.!"

I yelled something in return, I don't know what or why, which made Kinch throw a glance in my direction just as he cleared leather. But before he could bring the gun up, one of his boot soles slid on the metal slugs and he lost his balance, same as I had. He pitched backward against the press, then down onto his knees.

There's no telling what might have happened if he hadn't made the mistake of trying to lift himself upright by grabbing the edge of the form with his free hand. Artemas was there by then, and when he saw the form slide beneath the platen and Kinch still hanging on to it, he grabbed the chill arm and swung it hard and fast.

Kinch screamed loud and shrill when the heavy platen slammed down on his splayed fingers. The crushing pain made him drop the gun. I was on my feet by then and I scrambled over and got hold of it just as Artemas released the lever to let the platen snap back up. Kinch toppled over on his belly, clutching his mangled hand and moaning. The pain must have been fierce, but I wasn't in the least sorry for him after all he'd done and tried to do.

Artemas took the pistol from me and set it on the press. He had a cut on one cheek that was dribbling blood, but otherwise he didn't look to have been hurt in the fracas. He said, "Why didn't you do as I told you and stay put, R.W.? You might have got yourself shot."

"So might you."

"Well, then, we're both lucky."

The sound of running footfalls came from out in the alley, and Marshal Jennison burst through the door with his sidearm drawn. "Lord Almighty," he said when he saw the carnage.

Others had arrived, too. Homer, for one. And Dad, who pushed in past him and the marshal. He looked around, grimacing, and then picked his way over to me. "Are you all right, son?"

"Not hurt a bit," I said, though my head was throbbing some. "Thanks to Artemas."

"Thank God for that. But you shouldn't have chased down here."

"I guess I just acted without thinking."

The marshal had holstered his weapon and was leaning down to peer at Kinch moaning among the wreckage. "What happened to him?"

"He got his hand caught in the press," Artemas said.

"Dang bonehead. I clean forgot about him and his intention in all the excitement of the fire."

Dad said, "Intention? You knew this was going to happen, Seth?"

"Mary Beth come and told me earlier, but it wasn't supposed to happen until after midnight. I was fixing to set up a vigil and put a stop to it."

"How did Mary Beth know?"

"Overheard her father giving Kinch his orders."

"Naturally the Colonel was behind this outrage," Dad said furiously. "I want him arrested for malicious mischief, Seth—I want to see his miserable hide behind bars."

"He will be, don't worry none about that. But right now I got me a bunch of other fish to fry. Take Kinch to the jailhouse and fetch Doc Phillips for him. Make sure the fire's completely out. Arrest Jim Tarbeaux."

"Tarbeaux?" I said. "What for?"

"Setting fire to the saddle shop."

"You're wrong, Marshal," Artemas said. "He didn't set the fire."

"Sure he did. Rufus Cable seen him in the act and Bert Lawless seen him running away afterward."

"Lawless is mistaken. And Cable is lying."

"How the devil do you know that?"

Artemas sighed. "Because I seem to have a cussed knack for being in the neighborhood when trouble comes."

"Meaning what?"

"Meaning I saw Cable light the fire and run away afterward."

JIM TARBEAUX

I took Mary Beth to the Box Elder Hotel, to get her a room for the night, and then went looking for Marshal Jennison. I could have tried to speak to him at the fire, but he'd had his hands full and wouldn't have been in any frame of mind to listen to what I had to say. I wasn't eager to talk to him anyhow. What had happened tonight came down to my word against Cable's, same as five years ago. Maybe it'd be different this time, my word believed instead of his, but I wouldn't have wanted to bet on it.

I didn't have to go hunting the marshal; his deputy found me when I came out of the hotel. Dillard said little, just that I was to come along with him. Somewhat surprisingly, he led me upstreet to the Occidental House rather than to the jailhouse. Small groups of men who'd been watching the fire, and a couple of weary, smoke-grimed volunteers, were trooping in for a drink or two before going home, but we didn't follow them through the batwings into the saloon. Instead, we went around back through a door into Tate Reynolds's private office.

Several men were waiting there, all but one of them

standing, all but one with grim, set expressions. Marshal Jennison, Will Satterlee, Reynolds, banker and current mayor Frank Blevins, Bert Lawless who owned the lumberyard, a wide-eyed youngster in his teens, a yellow-haired, vaguely familiar fellow with ink-stained hands who looked as if he'd been in a fight. And Rufus Cable, the only one sitting, his face pale except for red splotches, his breath ragged and interrupted by coughs. He jumped up when he saw me, smoke-reddened eyes dark with hate, and pointed a finger and cried, "You did it, Tarbeaux! You burned my shop!"

"Like hell I did. You're the one who set that fire."

The marshal said, "Settle down, both of you. That's why we're all here, to get to the bottom of who done what." He added sardonically, "Not enough room at the jailhouse. Too many customers already."

"I keep telling you," Cable said, "I saw him do it, I *saw* him!"

"Let's hear your version, Tarbeaux. Were you in the saddle shop tonight?"

"I was. Cable came up to me in the street after I left your office earlier, asked me to meet him there in one hour."

"That's a lie! He—"

The marshal silenced him with a slicing gesture. "Why'd he want to wait an hour?"

"Said he needed time to settle his thoughts."

"Uh-huh. What was his reason for wanting to meet with you?"

"To talk, try to work things out between us."

"What things?"

"You know the answer to that," I said. "He stole the Kendalls' money five years ago, framed me for it—"

"Lies! Filthy lies!"

"Shut up, Rufus," Jennison said sharply. Then to me, "Go ahead."

"I didn't trust his motives, but I killed an hour and went to the shop to find out what he was up to. Never occurred to me he was desperate enough to set fire to his own place of business."

"Why would he do such a thing?"

"To frame me again. Have me sent back to prison so I wouldn't be a threat to him any longer."

"Afraid you'd kill him, like you said you would in court?"

"I never said that, not in so many words. That's not why I came back. All I wanted then and now is to clear my name."

"You tell him that?"

"Yes. Last week in his shop."

"Then why so afraid of you he'd frame you for arson?"

I told him why. Everything that had happened in Cable's shop that day last week, how he was dying from lung disease and had tried to force me to end his misery, that I'd made clear what my future intentions were. I finished up by saying, "I reckon he couldn't stand the prospect of having me around for the rest of his days, hounding him for a confession, reminding him of his guilt."

Mayor Blevins said, "He could have made an attempt on your life."

"He could have, but he's too much of a coward. The only way he could think to get rid of me was to burn his shop and blame me for it. But not before he saved some of his possessions."

"Why do you say that?"

"The saddle shop was about half empty when I went in there tonight. I noticed that just before he started the fire. A saddle and harness he'd had on display, some tools—all missing. He must've had this planned for days. My guess is you'll find the stuff stashed in his house."

"Maybe so," Jennison said. Then, "You were in the front part of the saddle shop when the fire started?"

I nodded. "I smelled kerosene just before. Cable must've spilled it all over the storeroom."

"What'd you do then?"

"Ran out, naturally. There was no way I could stop the fire from spreading."

The marshal turned to Bert Lawless. "You saw Tarbeaux come running out through the front door, that right, Bert?"

"That's right. I was on my way home from the lumberyard, like I told you before."

"And what part of the shop was ablaze? Front half?"

"No. No, the back half."

"What'd Tarbeaux do after he come out?"

"Ran down the alley toward the rear."

"To see if I could catch Cable," I said. "But he was gone by the time I got back there."

"See anybody else?"

"Yes, come to think of it. A man I didn't know came running past me shouting 'Fire!'" As soon as I said that, I realized who it had been. I pointed at the yellow-haired, ink-stained man. "Him."

"Jones," Will Satterlee said, "my printer, Artemas Jones."

"I'd been to the livery to collect some money Sam Benson had for me," Jones said, "and I was taking a shortcut through the alley when the back door of the saddle shop opened and this man here"—he nodded at Cable—"hurried out. He struck a match and pitched it back inside."

"You're sure it was Cable?"

"I'm sure. I had a good look at him in the firelight, and I'd seen him before when I tried to sell him a saddle. He ducked between two buildings when he saw me and I didn't know the area well enough to give chase. So I kept on going and sounded the alarm."

Through all of this Cable had remained silent, shaking his head brokenly, coughing in spasms, the hate in his eyes swallowed by fear. His legs had jellied enough so that he had to sit down again.

"Well, Rufus?" Jennison said to him. "You got anything to say for yourself?"

He didn't. He made a half-choking sound, his gaze roaming the faces of the others in the room. Grim, condemning faces like those of the jurymen at my trial. But this time, by God, the evidence was all against him and I was the one whose testimony was being believed, not his.

Justice done after all. Five years too late, but justice just the same.

SETH JENNISON

I'd been wrong about trouble coming in bunches lately. It'd come in bushels, by grab—more disorder, destruction, and lawlessness in one week than we'd had in the past five years. The jail was already three-quarters full, what with Rufus Cable and Jada Kinch and Al Yandle each occupying a cell, and if I'd had my druthers, which is to say the authority and jurisdiction, Colonel Elijah Greathouse would be looking out through the bars of the fourth. As it was, I'd wire the county sheriff and ask him to make tracks for the Square G with an arrest warrant as soon as he was able. The bars the Colonel would be looking out through then would be a cell in the county jail.

Fact was I'd about had my fill of devilment. If Box Elder didn't settle back down to being the mostly peaceable town it'd been before, I wouldn't stand for reelection come November. Let some other poor booger take over as marshal—and chairman of the annual Fourth of July celebration and head of the burial commission, the town council figuring it was better to pay one man a salary for wearing three different hats than three men salaries for wearing one apiece. Bert Lawless would take me on at the lumberyard, him and me being pretty close friends; and when it come time to retire, I could still spend my declining years guzzling beer and playing cribbage with the other codgers at the Odd Fellows Hall like I'd always planned on.

It'd been late when I finally crawled into bed and at that I hadn't slept well, so I was a mite late relieving Abner at the jailhouse and a mite grumpy when I did. It was another hot day, you could smell the smoke from last night's near disaster, and there was more noise than usual on account of the cleanup had already started. One botheration on top of another.

So happened I had a visitor waiting for me. Doc Christmas, all dressed up in his traveling duds. Well, I couldn't be grumpy toward him on account of the good deed him and Homer done in saving the newspaper office from total destruction, not to mention his unintentional good deed in ventilating Elrod Patch. I figured he'd come to say good-bye before they pulled out, which he had. But that wasn't all that was on his mind.

"It has been my experience," he said, "that a small-town law officer often keeps petty cash on hand, small amounts of which he is empowered by the city fathers to use for payment of services to the community. Is that true in your case, Marshal?"

"What if it is? What're you getting at, Doc?"

"The fact that Box Elder owes me three dollars."

"Three dollars? What in tarnation for?"

"Services rendered."

"Come again?"

"Services rendered," he said again. "My profession, as you well know, is primarily that of painless dentist, and secondarily the manufacture of Doc Christmas's Wonder Painkiller. I am particularly adept at ridding the mouths of my patients of badly decayed teeth. A town such as Box Elder, sir, is in many ways similar to the mouth of one of my suffering patients. It is healthy and harmonious only so long as its citizens . . . its individual teeth, if you will . . . are likewise healthy and harmonious. Several diseased teeth damage the entire mouth, as Box Elder has had the misfortune to be damaged recently. Elrod Patch was one of those diseased teeth, was he not?"

"Put it like that," I admitted, "I suppose he was."

"I did not extract him willingly from your midst, but the fact remains that I did extract him permanently, and with no harm whatsoever to the healthy teeth surrounding him. In effect, sir, painlessly. For a simple painless extraction I charge one dollar. You will agree, Marshal, that the extraction of Elrod Patch was not simple, but difficult. For difficult extractions I charge three dollars. Therefore, the town of Box Elder owes me three dollars for services rendered, payable on demand."

Well, if that didn't beat all. The doc had more gall than a trainload of politicians. If I'd been a lawyer, I reckon I could've come up with a good argument against his claim. But I'm not a lawyer, I'm a public servant. Besides which, my motto is, when a man's right he's right and there ain't no point in arguing with him.

On behalf of the healthy and harmonious teeth of Box Elder, I opened up the petty cash box and paid Doc Christmas his three dollars.

WILL SATTERLEE

It took R.W. and Artemas Jones half a day to gather up all the spilled types and quadrats, repair the damaged trays and frames and forms, sweep out the debris, and put the office back into a semblance of working order. Fortunately Jada Kinch had not had time to damage the Albion press.

While they were thus engaged, I stayed home and wrote furiously—long accounts of the vandalism, emphasizing the fact that Kinch had been acting on Colonel Greathouse's orders; the near-devastating fire set by Rufus Cable and his motive in doing so; and the parts Artemas Jones had played in bringing the miscreants in both cases to justice. I also rewrote my editorial to reflect these recent events. Whether or not the Colonel went to prison, his true colors had been revealed beyond any doubt and he would no longer be a powerful force in the basin. And whether or not Cable confessed to the theft of the Kendall money— Seth and I both thought he would eventually—his actions last night clearly established his guilt, thus restoring Jim Tarbeaux's good name and leaving Jim free to marry Mary

Beth no matter what her father or anyone else thought of the union.

As soon as I finished the copy, I took it to the *Banner* office. Jones and R.W. were almost done with their cleanup. I gave the copy to Artemas, who immediately took up his typestick and setting rule and went to work at his usual astonishing speed.

There had been so much eventful news since last week's issue that for the first time since my purchase of the *Banner* seven years ago, this week's special issue would run to six pages. The front page had to be completely remade, of course; Elrod's Patch's demise was no longer of primary importance. I decided that the fire and its aftermath should be the lead story, under full four-column banner and subheads, with the assault on our shop as the secondary lead. Together, the stories would take up the entire front page, with continuation on page two. That page and all except what would now be page six needed to be remade as well, and the two additional pages added. My account of Doc Christmas's self-defense shooting of Patch, as it turned out, was relegated to page three.

When Jones finished setting the two lead stories, he said somewhat ruefully, "You sure did give me a lot of ink, Mr. Satterlee, much more than I deserve."

"Not to my way of thinking. If it hadn't been for you, Kinch would surely have created even more havoc here, perhaps irreparably broken the press, and Jim Tarbeaux would be in jail instead of Rufus Cable."

R.W. chimed in, "Now we know firsthand how you earned your nickname, Artemas."

"Earned it? Blind luck, if you ask me."

The three of us worked tirelessly the rest of that day and half the next. It was necessary for me to somewhat alter my account of the criminal trespass—which I did with great satisfaction—when Seth Jennison delivered word that Colonel Greathouse had been arrested by the county sheriff on a charge of suborning the wanton destruction of private property. The press run was our largest ever, three hundred copies instead of the usual two hundred.

Well-wishers interrupted us now and then, and more came around to shake Jones's hand and pat him on the back. He seemed embarrassed by all the attention. I judged it was because he was a private man who shunned the limelight, and that he was uncomfortable in a hero's role. "Give-a-Damn" was certainly an appropriate moniker, as R.W. had stated, but it was my impression that Jones considered it less a badge of honor, as most men would have, than a cross he was forced to bear.

This was borne out the day after the *Banner*'s special issue appeared. Upon closing the office the night before I had paid Jones his week's wages, including a bonus of twenty-five dollars which he accepted gratefully and without reluctance. I learned later that he spent most of it that night, playing stud poker at the Free and Easy saloon, and in Tillie Johnson's parlor house—activities which under normal circumstances I do not approve of. Profligacy was not the reason he failed to show up at the *Banner* office in the morning, however. Sometime in the dawn hours he had packed his bindle and departed on a Great Northern freight for parts unknown.

He said nothing to me, nor to R.W. to the boy's chagrin, about moving on. He was not a man for good-byes, any more than a man for praise or conceit or sentiment. There one day, gone the next. True to himself, his calling, his pleasures, and his principles in every way.

I had known that he would leave soon, but I was sorry he was gone. Tramp printers are a dime a dozen, and none before had left me with a feeling of regret when they departed. But Give-a-Damn Jones was no ordinary itinerant typesetter, and I—and R.W. and not a few others in Box Elder—would not soon forget him.

ON THE ROAD

OWEN HAZARD

It was more than a year and a half before my path crossed Give-a-Damn Jones's again. That happy occasion took place in Dubuque, Iowa, a town known for lead mining, lumber mills, and Mississippi River traffic, where I happened to be hand-pegging for the *Telegraph*. The paper had a deserved reputation as a haven of refuge for itinerant typesetters, none of our breed ever having been refused work in its composing room.

It was said on the road that the citizenry of Dubuque were always ready for fight, frolic, or footrace, and I was finding that to be true. The town was nowhere near as wide open as Butte and some others, but there were plenty of the usual kinds of amusement, plus horse racing at Lake Peosta and prizefighting at Eagle Point on the Wisconsin side of the river. The favorite watering hole of printers was a saloon in Bee Town owned by a gent named Nick Denney, whose brother was in the trade. All you had to do to get a drink there was lay a printer's rule on the bar. I was in Nick's place one evening, playing euchre and drinking beer, when Jones walked in.

Well, he was sure a sight for sore eyes. I'd heard plenty about him since we'd parted company in Butte—a legend on the road growing grander all the time, that was Give-a-Damn Jones. Still attracting trouble like a dish of honey attracts flies and doing his good deeds everywhere he went, big city and small town. According to the grapevine he'd foiled a bank robbery in Kansas City, shot a card cheat in St. Louis, saved a widow from losing five thousand dollars to a confidence man in Peoria, and had a whole passel of adventures while working on a jim-crow sheet in eastern Montana not long after leaving Butte.

Some of that was surely exaggeration, if not fabrication—no man, not even Jones, could have done all those good turns without a dime novelist such as Ned Buntline finding out about it and writing a book or three about his exploits. But after watching him in action in Butte, the night he'd stopped the drunk from beating up the Chinese prostitute, I had no doubt that some of all that was said about him was true to one degree or another.

He was as glad to see me as I was to see him. He hadn't changed a bit, far as I could tell, except for a few more lines etched into his craggy face and a touch of gray in his yellow hair. He was looking for work, so I took him over to the *Telegraph* and introduced him to the composing-room foreman. The foreman had heard of him—hell, who in the printing trade hadn't?—and handed him a rule on the spot.

Jones and me took up where we'd left off a year and half ago, doing some carousing in Nick's place, the other saloons, a couple of bordellos, and up at Lake Peosta. Naturally we traded yarns about our days on the road since we'd last seen each other, but he was still reticent about discussing his penchant—he called it his "curse"—for trouble. I was too curious about the latest batch of rumors to let 'em be for long—especially the one about his experiences in that eastern Montana town, Box Elder. So one night in Nick's, after we'd both downed half a dozen glasses of applejack, a tipple I'd learned to like and Jones found just as palatable and that has a way of loosening tongues, I brought up the subject kind of roundabout.

"Tell me, Artemas, you win any more horses in poker games?"

"Hell, no. I'll never place another bet when there's anything but money in the pot. I'm all through with horses."

"Heard you rode the one you won in Butte to a town called Box Elder and got mixed up in all sorts of wild doings there."

He scowled at me over the rim of his glass. "Just what exactly did you hear?"

"That you did so much for the folks there they all but put up a statue in your honor. Captured an arsonist, saved their newspaper office from being torn apart, brained the town bully and then maybe had a hand in him getting shot in self-defense, and cleared an ex-con's reputation so he could marry his sweetheart."

Give-a-Damn's scowl got even darker. "Didn't I tell you

once not to believe everything you hear about me, that most of it's sheep dip?"

"Not all that happened in Box Elder, though."

"No? What makes you think not?"

"Pop Cowan—you remember him—he showed me part of a special issue of the *Box Elder Banner* he got somewhere that told all about it. Your name might as well have been writ in boldface."

"Listen here, Owen. A traveling dentist named Doc Christmas shot the bully in self-defense, just like it said he did. I wasn't anywhere near, didn't have a thing to do with it."

"What about the rest?"

"Exaggeration, plain and simple. Paper's owner, Will Satterlee, was prone to writing with a pen dipped in hyperbolic ink."

"That doesn't answer my question," I said. "Did you brain that bully with a beer glass before he got killed, saving the life of a farm boy the bully was about to break in two?"

Give-a-Damn snorted. "Big oaf swung an arm at me while the two of them were fighting, I swung back. That's all there was to it."

"Capture an arsonist that set fire to half the town?"

"No. And it wasn't half the town that burned, it was four buildings."

"Save the newspaper office from being destroyed?"

"No again. It was mostly torn up by the time I got there,

and Satterlee's son and I were lucky not to've got shot by the fool that did the damage."

"Clear the ex-con's reputation so he could marry his sweetheart?"

"Didn't happen. I only met him once, and never laid eyes on the woman."

"Well, then. So you weren't a hero in Box Elder after all."

"Hah."

"Didn't keep finding yourself in the right place at the right time?"

"Wrong place at the wrong time. And no, I wasn't any hero. I'd give a year's pay never to be called one again."

"What about the time you were working in Kansas City? Word is you foiled a bank robbery there."

"Sheep dip!" Give-a-Damn said, and hollered to Nick for another round of applejack.